one big echo of a
much nicer place

PUBLISHED BY SCRYFA

DESIGNED AND EDITED BY SIMON PARKER

COVER: TREWIDDEN NIGHT BY ROD WALKER

© MARTIN PHILP 2009 © SCRYFA
ISBN 978-0-9552869-9-5

PRINTED BY HEADLAND IN CORNWALL

MARTIN PHILP IS FROM HAYLE IN CORNWALL
SEVERAL OF HIS STORIES HAVE APPEARED IN *SCRYFA*

ONE BIG ECHO OF A MUCH NICER PLACE IS HIS FIRST BOOK

HE WISHES TO THANK HIS MUM, DAD, HELEN AND GARGI FOR READING
THESE STORIES AND PASSING ON THEIR USEFUL COMMENTS,
ROD WALKER FOR THE USE OF HIS COVER PAINTING
AND SIMON PARKER FOR HIS TIME, GENEROSITY AND
ENTHUSIASM WHILE PUTTING THIS COLLECTION TOGETHER

contents

merry fucking christmas

JACK TREMENYANS hurtled through the skylight and landed on his coccyx in a mound of golden tinsel, a net of lights falling close behind and bagging him so completely it was a good minute of struggling and groaning before he could free himself from the festive trap and plunge his hand down his drawers to fondle his aching arse.

'Merry Christmas, Jack,' said Councillor Simons, walking by with a slim portfolio under his arm and a sly grin on his face.

'Merry Christmas?' said Jack. 'I'll give you merry fucking Christmas.'

And Councillor Simons, Conservative, walked on towards the chamber and felt a warm mince pie glow topped with a sweet dusting of seasonal goodwill; and he even smiled at Tony Keth, Ragged Trousered Philanthropist from Penzance North.

And why wouldn't he? After all, Jack Tremenyans' festive expletives were the first real sign of the season to come: yes there were premature TV advertisements and early displays in department stores, but it was an unspoken agreement among those in the know that the season of good cheer was truly upon you with Jack's Merry Fucking Christmas.

Jack struggled free from the net of lights, climbed up the ladder and pulled down more boxes from the eaves of St John's Hall, all the time working on a few choice variations of his favourite catchphrase.

'I'll give you effing Christmas,' he muttered.

Which was apt, for if by 'you' Jack meant the good

citizens of Penzance then he certainly did give them Christmas. With jingle bells on. For 20 years – since 1967 – the cantankerous old socialist had cursed his way up Market Jew Street and Causewayhead, then down Chapel Street, decorating the town until it dripped with seasonal colour. And as the years rolled by and Jack became a familiar sight, his effing and blinding became, oddly, as heartwarming a part of the Christmas season as the illuminated results of his labours.

Jack hated Christmas, of course. Absolutely hated it. True, in the old days he had consulted his trenchant left-wing views and found a place for it, albeit begrudgingly, as a peculiar and overritualised expression of the brotherhood of man (weren't there Christian Socialists, after all?). But these days, with its gorged celebrants, drunkenness and too many toys for the kids, it was all vulgarity and greed. An offshoot of Thatcherism, if you like. And Jack? What was he doing? He was effing his way up one end of town and blinding it down the other, preparing Penzance for the gluttonous celebrations at the heart of modern capitalism.

Jack also hated Christmas and his part in its preparations because of the physical pain involved. Like the moth to the flame the clumsy man is drawn to ladders, hammers and electricity, and so it was with Jack. He was Harold Lloyd and Laurel and Hardy all rolled into one, banging his thumb and screeching so loud it itched the ears of passers-by; diving into oncoming traffic as a string of lights – like a nest of Tory vipers – tripped him; and, yes, on one occasion scrambling up a falling ladder to clutch a streetlight, his panic so intense he surely defied the laws of gravity to save himself.

Everyone loved Jack. Even the Tories. And when his thumb-banging, hurtling and cursing was finished, Penzance had a display to put bigger places such as Truro to shame. The town glittered like a kindly old prostitute, the crack and crumble of her main streets lost in shiny baubles. It was a happy scene that obscured the grey decay of a Cornish winter for a few weeks. And people thanked Jack for it, too. When he had completed his last precarious duties on the Market House, they put their arms around his tired shoulders, led him across the road to The Star and bought him drinks. And as the smoky air hit him and the cheers and indulgent laughter warmed his tired old body, he would slump in a chair and shake his head. And say: 'Ladders, ledges, roofs – I'm up and down like a bride's nightie and I don't even like Christmas. Why in Christ's name do I do it?'

But he fooled no one. Which is why no one said: Why don't you give it up, Jack? It's voluntary work and you're not getting paid.

No, no one asked because it was common knowledge that hating Christmas and its accompanying labours were the single happy event in the barren calendar of a lonely old bachelor.

***

'I approached the store room,' said Sheila Mitchell, Mayor of Penzance and leader of Penwith District Council, 'and heard the most dreadful language.'

'Oh dear, no,' said deputy leader Terry Maddern.

'Awful language. To think one is preparing to meet public dignitaries and carry out the necessary business of office and should be treated to coarsities about Jesus, Mary, Joseph and the three wise men.'

'I think I can explain,' said Terry.

Sheila ignored him. 'So I poked my head around the door and there was a dishevelled man with bloodshot eyes draped in lights and tinsel. "What on earth do you think you're doing?" I said. The man looked startled for a moment, then he said, "I wish in God's name I knew myself." Then he held up a banner of the three wise men and said, "These bastards" – I'm sorry Terry, to use such language – "These bastards were clever enough to perform their great labours just the one Christmas. Old Dickhead here," he said, poking his finger in his chest, "He does it every effing year."'

'Awful,' said Terry, shaking his head and biting into his beard. 'Very upsetting. But the thing is, Sheila, Jack is a much loved character in Penzance. Being a St Ives woman you perhaps wouldn't realise he's something of an institution.'

'Institution?' said Sheila, holding her chain of office to her face as a mirror and straightening her hair. 'The man should be in an institution.'

And Sheila and Terry went on to their meeting and that would have been that. If only the right worshipful lady hadn't popped into town the following day to do a bit of Christmas shopping and seen Jack in full flow.

***

It was a cold day in early December and Sheila Mitchell strolled up Market Jew Street, her lips curled into something akin to a smile. The musty odour of a cluster of charity shops limped out into the street and crept up her nostrils. She held her breath and hurried on. Shiny pastry fare leered at her through the window of the bakery. Customers looked out blankly from the Nice Bit Of Sit Down Cafe, an awful place where mothers surrounded by plastic bags sucked on cigarettes, like refugees with all their worldly belongings.

A dreadful place. Even Humphry Davy at the top of Market Jew Street seemed to agree, his hand on his hip and a look of haughty condescension that said: It's about time you dreadful people pulled yourselves together and made something of your lives.

No, Sheila didn't like Penzance. And if Anthony didn't have his practice in Penzance, and if the machinations of a Tory campaign machine had not seen this relative newcomer elected Mayor of Penzance and chairwoman of Penwith District Council in record time, she would quite happily return to St Ives and visit only for essential provisions. In the circumstances, Sheila settled for second best and made it her duty to avoid the town centre and its folk as often as possible, for to meet either was a reminder that attaining the highest office in this place meant nothing more than presiding over the lives of a very sorry community.

And wasn't there a certain futility, thought Sheila, as she remembered a recent site meeting on a sunny Monday afternoon in Penlee Street, in fighting heatedly for the rejection of a planning application that would deny a man light, when the very man who lodged the objection answered the door to local government officers and councillors in a dressing gown, fag and can of strong lager in hand, and led them into a dank living room that had heard not the faintest rumour of the crisp winter day outside?

No, thought Sheila, as she reached the top of Market Jew Street and turned into Causewayhead, as a Penzance person would no doubt say, you can't shine…

'Shit!'

Sheila stopped. A small crowd had gathered outside the shoe shop.

'Christ Almighty!'

She looked up towards the source of the expletives. And there hovered Jack Tremenyans, one foot on ladder, the other on roof of shop, his arms and legs a hopeless

9

tangle of wires and bulbs. A diabolical tangle, actually, and with too much mischief to be a random arrangement. Because somehow the spirit of corporate Christmas, which hated Jack as much as he hated it, had arranged the wires and bulbs so beautifully they made both puppet and puppeteer out of him, so that should he lift his left arm, his left leg followed, and should he attempt to ground himself better on the roof with his right leg, his left went with it and threatened to step away from the ladder into thin air.

Jack struggled and struggled to untangle himself but only seemed to get further caught up. Meanwhile the crowd had grown larger, a mass of enraptured citizens who had now completely forgotten to put the dinner on or pick up the kids from school as they watched the precariously perched puppet and puppeteer above.

Jack stopped struggling and looked down at the crowd.

'Merry Christmas, Jack,' shouted Percy Johns.

'Merry Christmas?' said Jack. 'I'll give you merry fucking Christmas.'

And, to illustrate the unmerriness of the Christmas period, Jack threw his left arm up in the air with an angry gesture. Which was unfortunate, because Jack's left leg was compelled to go with it. A strange figure Jack made, with his left arm above his head, left leg bent at the knee. An obscure Tai Chi movement, perhaps? Not for idiosyncratic Jack a commonplace Carry Tiger and Return to Mountain or Step Back and Repulse Monkey, but the esoteric Show Anger at Festive Duties by Teetering on Roof on One Leg.

Because, of course, Jack was on one leg now, and demanding far too much from it. An affront to the laws of physics, you could say, that haggard old body hanging in the air with only a sloping roof as grounding. A miracle. And yet a brief one, for in truth it was perhaps no more than a second that he hung there before gravity, piqued from its slumber by the sharp intakes of breath and laughter from the assembled crowd below, brought its full force into play.

And if Jack fought valiantly from this moment on, there was something as inevitable as the laws of physics in his descent.

'Arseholes,' he said as his foot slid from the roof towards the guttering, snapped through the guttering and continued its journey south. 'Bastards,' he said as his right arm clutched at the guttering, slowing his journey but never likely to save him from the crunch of flesh and bone on pavement. The crowd turned and scattered to the edges of the street as Jack, followed by ladder and tools, headed towards them.

And so it was a mystery to hear the clatter of aluminium ladder and the brittle ring of tools hitting block paving. But no sickening crunch of Jack.

The crowd looked up. A miracle. Well, no not a miracle because... well, yes a miracle actually. There was Jack, spread-eagled, hanging in the air. And if not defeating gravity then offering it a severe setback because at his wrists, ankles and midriff a web of wires connected him to the shoe shop roof on one side of the street and the butcher's on the other. The puppet who was his own puppeteer was now the spider caught in a web of his own making. Jack looked down at the astonished people of Penzance.

'Every year,' he said, scanning the crowd. 'Every bastard year I go through these shenanigans for a shower of shit like you lot.' He shook his head and swayed in his web. 'Why I bother I shall never know.'

'Merry Christmas, Jack.' It was Percy Johns again, grinning.

And people shifted from foot to foot with expectation and waited. And who would have thought it possible that Jack would muster a festive outburst so coarse and creative – never had the virginity of Mary been so evocatively doubted – that it put even his roof-stumbling antics in the shade and would be remembered for years to come?

***

Sheila Mitchell was incensed. Jack Tremenyans was the very mascot of vulgarity and civic incompetence, and advertised to the world at large the failure of Penzance. She decided he must go.

Sheila was one of those people who is most resolute when they know they can get someone else to do their dirty work for them. So, when the issue of Jack was raised in private with a select group of councillors, she shouted down the doubters with the utmost conviction and stated most firmly that he would play no further part in putting up the Christmas lights.

What was there to doubt? Well, all could see her point, but it was Draconian, cruel even, to deny Jack his yearly labours. Even more to the point – and it was the ever-pragmatic Councillor Simons who raised this issue – who would tell the poor sod?

'Don't you worry about that,' said Sheila, waving away such a trifling concern.

And they were all impressed by her willingness to see this decision through to its conclusion, despite a necessary meeting with Jack that would surely provoke much anger and sorrow.

To be fair, Deputy Leader Terry Maddern was less impressed when he discovered it was not Sheila who would do the dirty deed but him.

'It makes perfect sense,' said Sheila. 'You've known this dreadful man far longer than I have. He'll take it better from you.'

Terry was nodding, something he did with great vigour when he strongly disagreed with someone. The nodding slowly came to a halt. Next he lifted his right index finger and pressed it over his lips. He was thinking, you see, considering. It did not make perfect sense to Terry that a man who had neither the conviction nor good reason to relieve poor Jack of his duties should be the one to break the bad news to him. No sense at all. On the other hand, Terry was afraid of Sheila and she was his superior: with that consideration in mind it most certainly made sense. It was a simple coward's decision. A reflex choice. And yet Terry struck his finger-to-lips pose for far longer than was necessary, his lidded eyes staring at the floor so as not to offer distraction to a mind that was apparently so wise and just in its workings it could surely trace some lineage back to celebrated Jewish kings. A marvellous performance, it was, and one that generally helped Terry retain some shred of self respect in the wake of his submissiveness. Should Sheila have asked him to ramraid Curry's and make off with TV sets, or introduce compulsory Chinese burns to primary school children, Terry would have made his decision in a moment, then appear to cogitate with such force that impressionable citizens might well have decided that someone who had thought about it so marvellously must be right to agree ramraiding or inflicting Chinese burns was, indeed, a sensible proposal.

Sheila, however, wasn't fooled.

'Just tell him it's a health and safety thing,' she said, walking towards the chamber in the middle of the performance. Terry nodded, his eyes still on the floor, his finger still rigid over pursed lips, the pose all the more authentic now as he deliberated on how he would break the news to Jack Tremenyans.

***

Terry popped his head around the storeroom door and grinned.

'Can I have a word?'

Jack looked up. He was sitting on the floor surrounded by mounds of bulbs arranged in piles of green, red and yellow.

'Do you know how many of these bastard things I change every Christmas?

Terry shook his head.

'More than 300,' said Jack. 'So, no, Terry, if you bastards want a bloody Christmas this year, you can't have a word – I'm running myself ragged putting up these buggers.'

Terry saw his chance and stepped into the room.

'That's exactly what I need to talk to you about. There's been a bit of discussion and everyone agrees we've been expecting far too much from you and it isn't fair.'

'Not fair?' Jack leaned back against the wall and hooted with laughter. 'You had one of your sub-select committees in your suits and ties with your madam chairman to work out it isn't fair? It's never been fair, Terry, all the running around I do for this town. But then, life's not fair or we wouldn't have a chamberful of bastard Tories like you lot running the council, would we?'

And Jack, who was in an unusually good mood, was so shaken by his laughter he had to rest a palm on the ground to support himself.

'Arseholes,' he said.

Jack winced and held up his palm, a mess of blood and broken glass.

Terry, solicitous Terry, hurried towards him with a fresh hanky.

'Thank you, boy, but it's nothing,' said Jack, patting his hand on his trousers.

'But it is,' said Terry, knees bent and hovering over Jack. 'Times are changing. We're living in a very litigious age. One of your accidents could cost this council a fortune.'

'Mishaps,' said Jack sucking his palm. 'Not accidents.'

'Whatever you want to call them, it all adds up to negligence. It could be a terrible blow for the taxpayers of Penzance.'

Jack looked up at Terry, who was hovering and grinning above him. 'What are you trying to say, boy?'

'It's what I came to talk to you about. It might be time to call it a day.'

Jack dropped his palm from his face and smiled. His mouth was covered in blood. 'Call it a day? And who will put on Christmas this year? Santa's little helpers?'

'Everyone appreciates the hard work you've done, but we'll all muck in and carry on as best we can.'

Jack shook his head. 'And a right balls-up you'd make of it, too. No. Thank you, Terry, but we shall have to carry on as we are.' He jabbed himself in the chest. 'Old Dickhead here performs labours at Christmas to put Mary herself to shame. I don't know why, but I do. And I don't complain.'

Terry was in a bit of a quandary. No matter how strongly he hinted to Jack that his time was up, Jack refused to take the bait. Fortunately for Terry, when he wasn't scared or intimidated by someone, he could make genuine decisions powered by his own volition.

Unfortunately for those around him, they had nothing of the wisdom of Solomon about them. In this case he decided a cup of tea or a softly softly approach would not work: moving in for the kill now was the kindest thing to do.

'No, Jack, I insist,' he said, reaching down and untangling a string of lights. 'We've expected too much from you and with health and safety concerns on top of it all, we've decided to do the decent thing.' Terry dropped the bulbs and stood up straight. 'I won't hear another word about it. You can call it a day once you've sorted out your bulbs.'

Jack grinned at Terry. He didn't say anything, he just watched him for a long time. Terry spread his legs a little wider, put his hands behind his back and stared down at the ground.

'You don't look like you're going to take no for an answer,' said Jack quietly.

'It's a unanimous decision.'

'Unanimous?'

'All of us.'

'I know what it means.' Jack smiled. 'Well, thank Christ for that.' He shook his head. His eyes were glassy. He began sorting his bulbs once more. 'At last I can have a bit of peace and quiet.'

***

'Thank Christ for that.'

Jack shook his head and repeated the words several times, walking past the antique shops and glowing pubs of Chapel Street as the thin winter light faded into dusk.

'A bit of peace and quiet at last,' he said as he looked in the window of the Admiral Benbow, the small bar bursting with brass and beards and smiling faces.

He headed along the promenade, listening to waves crashing on slippery black rocks in the darkness below.

'Free to do just as I please,' he called out to the ocean, for though Jack was not an aesthete, he could sense the shot widening and his own small soul – so busy, always so busy at Christmas – getting lost in a larger and larger landscape. The world was getting bigger and bigger, more cavernous: Jack had to fill it with words, with something.

At home he made a ham and mustard sandwich and sat at the dining room table, masticating slowly and sighing with apparent contentment at his new-found freedom. Then he sat on the settee and switched on the box. He turned up his milky old eyes and tutted. It was a gameshow hosted by Jeremy Noah, that little fart with the curly hair and tidy beard. That smug Tory shit. Jack shifted in his seat and rooted around his mouth for any lingering bits of bread. He could tell a Tory a mile off. They smiled. Even when they weren't happy or amused they smiled, warding off the fatal error of earnestness, of decency. A Tory must approach the world with sly amusement, with glibness and irony; kind words were just words, tactics in the greater war, the struggle between man and man. A Tory touched by earnestness would crumble to dust like a vampire speared by a shaft of daylight. Jack hated them. Hated this little fart on the screen for condescending to working people; hated Terry Maddern for his unctuous insincerities about giving Jack a break; hated Sheila Mitchell for the polished snobbery that put appearances and self-promotion over community and decency.

The gameshow ended. Jack's anger faded. He smiled. People thought he was coarse and stupid; they laughed at him. But he could see through the likes of Terry Maddern and her bloody worship Sheila Mitchell with her chains of office. And yet it had all come to good. Because Jack – yes, Jack the atheist, the socialist – had been up and down bloody ladders for 20 years. And now he could please himself and have a nice bit of rest.

He dropped his head back and sighed. He looked around the room. Not a great man for decorating or prettifying, Jack; utilitarian purpose was the order of the day in the Tremenyans household. And yet there were the photos: Jack holding hands with Charlie and Emma, his sister Vera's kids; Mother and Father bewildered in Trafalgar Square on their one and only trip to London in 1951; Jack shaking hands with Reginald King, Chairman of the Transport and General Workers Union.

Jack sighed again. Not much to show for a life of graft. But then, in Jack's day, you were thankful for the essentials; anything else was a bonus.

And yet wasn't everything Jack did unnecessary since his retirement? He drummed his fingers on the settee and rooted around his mouth for bread once more. But it was all gone. His mouth was empty, his house was empty, the promenade was empty and, Jesus H Christ, Jack was a doer and he had to do something even if it was useless and pointless.

He sprang up from the settee, strode into the hall and snatched the attic pole. Then, cursing under his breath, he jabbed the pole at the ceiling and hooked the attic door. Jack gave it an angry pull, the door tilted and down came the ladder, well oiled, silent and devastating as it extended and fell towards the floor.

And landed on Jack's foot.

'Christ all fucking Mighty!'

Jack limped up the ladder and rustled about in the attic. Bin bags tumbled into the hall. Jack came back down the ladder and dragged the bags into the living room.

'Someone's got to do it,' said Jack, muttering under his breath. 'And if I don't, no bugger will.'

Of course, what was to be done did not need doing at all, unless you consider gaffer-taping lonely moments to endless unnecessary tasks a genuine necessity. Because Jack – the atheist, the socialist, the anti-consumerist – was putting up a plastic Christmas tree.

A marvellous job he did, too. Jack was in his element now, cursing at stringless baubles – how in Christ's name were you meant to hang a bauble without string? – tripping over tinsel and searching for the one defective bulb in a string of 120 lights with an elaborate defamation of the bulb's character that surely would have convinced any witness it was sentient, could hear Jack loud and clear, voted Conservative and was hiding from his trembling fingers out of sheer malice.

Jack finished. The tree looked beautiful. He shook his head and smiled. Then something odd happened. Jack's face, glowing in festive pink, yellow and green, twinkled with its own little festive bauble: a tear, growing in the corner of his eye and hanging for a moment, before bursting and falling down his haggard old face.

***

Sheila was glad to be rid of Jack, but it quickly became apparent that the good people of Penzance were backward in coming forward when it came to helping put the lights up. Days passed. December arrived. The opening ceremony had to be put back. Jack's decorations, half completed, hung like cobwebs over the town.

Sheila and Terry were desperate. They – or rather Terry – implored anyone who would listen, Terry lecturing binmen, street cleaners and anyone remotely connected to the local authority payroll of their civic responsibilities. It was then they learned the truth: the people of Penzance thought they were a couple of shithouses for getting rid of Jack, and would not lift a finger to help. Even fellow Tories were not prepared to lend a hand.

'But I will have a word with the great man himself,' said Councillor Robbie Simons.

'Ask him back?' said Terry.

'Unless you have any better ideas?'

'Never,' said Sheila. 'Penzance is better off in darkness.'

'Darkness it is then,' said Robbie with a grin, thoroughly enjoying the shit creek his fellow councillors were palming their way up. Socialist or not, Jack was a good sort: and what was Christmas without that cantankerous old bastard?

A week passed. No one came forward. It rained, as it often did in Penzance in December. And yet on previous years, as night fell, the illuminated lights and decorations shone above and made strange shiver reflections in the greasy street below. And Penzance looked quite beautiful. But not this year. No, 1987 was the year of the streetlight illuminations, relentless, fascistic almost in their uniform spacing and unsentimental glare, compelling the townsfolk forward – move along, move along – into bleak January. Still no one came forward. The town held out against Sheila and Terry.

It was a troubled time for all – except for the editorial staff of *The Buccaneer*, who enjoyed an unusually fertile creative period coming up with appropriate headlines including 'No light at end of tunnel for Penzance', 'Let there be light!' (a covert plea to Sheila Mitchell to reinstate Jack, perhaps?) and 'Dark days for Penzance traders'. It was the latter that got Sheila's attention and made her realise this was more than a minor dispute over a festive display: the lack of lights in the town was keeping people away in their droves. The first late-night shopping – it was the first week of December now – was a disaster, the shops fluorescent and empty, staff slumped against tills or idling about the aisles, the businesses of Market Jew Street Edward Hopper tableaux of loneliness and urban alienation instead of the lively jostle, bustle and tinkle of tills that warmed retailers' hearts.

It was costing the good middle class shopkeepers of Penzance money; and, since Sheila was openly implicated in the removal of Jack Tremenyans, that would cost Sheila votes in the May elections.

'Tell Councillor Simons he can have his word with the awful man,' said Sheila. 'Only he must make clear there will be no more swearing or tomfoolery. He can put up his decorations, but he will put them up quietly or not at all.'

***

Councillor Simons walked across the Promenade, grinning to himself as his suit flapped in the cold wind coming off the sea. He was looking forward to the torrent of abuse he could expect from Jack; it was a source of great pleasure to watch the old bastard puff himself up, pointing just over Councillor Simons' shoulder, his eyes fixed on a point just over that shoulder too, and castigate the vile Tory's evil ways. He would not point or look directly at Councillor Simons, you see, only past him. For if he happened to meet the wretched Tory's eye, which he inevitably did as Councillor Simons manoeuvred into view, the leathery parchment of Jack's face, scrawled with socialist invective in angry lines and frowns, would unfurl and a smile would ruin everything.

It was impossible not to like Councillor Simons, even for Jack. Yes he was a Tory, but he seemed to possess all the good, fun bits about being a Tory and few of the bad ones. He had maverick ideas, he pronounced profanities against the social contract with a devilish grin, he winked at female councillors across the chamber. He lived in the social vacuum of pure Toryness, his personality not tethered to his fellow men and women in considerations of responsibility and appropriate action; and therefore he was a kind of eternal bachelor, an über bachelor, married neither to a woman nor his fellow townsfolk. Even responsible socialists like Jack could look at him with envy as he loitered about the town with his carefree charm, bartering down the price of joints and fillets with sour-faced butchers and fishmongers; or, leaning with one foot on a bench, elbow on knee, tailored suit riding up his forearm, smoked a cigarette and chatted to passers-by with the air of a man who may revel in the time on his hands because other people are making his money for him.

He knocked on Jack's door.

A haggard face peered through the warped glass. The door opened.

'You?' he said, to a point past Councillor Simons' left shoulder. 'What in Christ's name do you want?'

Councillor Simons grinned.

'Good news. They want you back.'

'Bad news. They can eff off.'

'Can I come in?'

Jack disappeared into the cottage gloom and Councillor Simons followed. Jack made tea and plonked the biscuit barrel on the coffee table between them. Councillor Simons poked through the rich teas and

digestives and helped himself to two
Penguin.

'They're desperate,' he said.

'I can see that.'

'It's like this. Providing you behave in a way befits a representative of the council, you're back in charge.'

'Tug my forelock?' said Jack. 'Bastards!'

'Not at all. It's the effing and the blinding Sheila objects to. She thinks it lowers the tone.'

'Lowers the tone?' Jack shot up and cleared his throat. 'They're up there,' he said, pointing at the standard lamp (presumably the council chamber lay beyond), 'lining their fucking pockets. Tory councillors awarding council contracts to fellow Tory councillors, Tory councillors building bungalows in Areas of Outstanding Natural Beauty because fellow Tories on the planning committee give the say so. I know it all. Everyone knows it. They look after their own. But, presumably, it's all right to be rotten to your bastard core as long as you smile nicely and don't slurp your soup at the table. And me' – Jack jabbed himself in the chest – 'I live an honest life, I've drawn an honest wage and I've worked selflessly for the people of this town, without thinking about making myself a nest egg with taxpayers' money. And because I use a bit of colourful language, because I express myself honestly and eff and blind when I get upset, they bastards' – Jack threw his arm towards the standard lamp and glared at the spartan object as if it were decked in jewels and furs – 'They – corrupt – bastard – Tories – don't – like – it. Well fuck them. I wouldn't take the job back now if they said: "Jack, you can eff and blind till kingdom come."'

He sat back down, plunged his hand into the biscuit barrel and pulled out an honest working-class digestive.

..., munching on the biscuit, he caught Councillor Simons' eye, shook his head and began to chuckle despite himself.

'Anyway,' he said. 'I'm happy. It's a blessed relief to be done with lights and banners and bloody ladders.'

'There's nothing I could say to change your mind?'

Jack shook his head.

They sat in silence. Councillor Simons looked around the gloomy, cramped cottage, with its chipboard furniture, plastic settee and functional gloom and thought of his own bachelor front room with the oak coffee table, deep leather sofa and masculine furnishings that rose ceilingward and shone in silvers and metal greys. He bowed his head and paid respect to the simplicity of Jack's life, and felt sorry that the mean-spirited Sheila Mitchell had denied the man his source of joy because of her sourness and priggery. Councillor Simons gazed into Jack's Christmas tree. It was rudely laden with tinsel, baubles and flashing lights, and oddly out of keeping with the rest of the room.

He smiled.

'I have an idea.' He reached into the biscuit barrel and pulled out another Yo-yo. 'What if you went back to work and finished the job, nice and quietly just as Sheila asks.'

Jack began to interrupt. Councillor Simons held up his hand.

'But then, on Switching On Night, you get to address the crowd in your own inimitable way.'

'They haven't let me on that platform in 20 years. In fact, none of those Tory bastards have even thanked me in 20 years.'

'I'm not talking about the platform or thanks for your hard work,' said Councillor Simons, unwrapping his Yo-yo. 'I'm talking about something far better.' He looked at Jack's tree and grinned. 'Jack, this is the Christmas Penzance will never forget.' He rolled the foil wrapper into a ball and flicked it into the biscuit barrel.

'And you, old friend, you're going to be a legend.'

***

Jack returned to work. And it was a joy to the townspeople of Penzance to see the haggard old bastard up his ladder again. But a brief joy. Because Jack was different now. He didn't eff and blind and his Laurel and Hardy moments were few and far between. People said that Sheila Mitchell had crushed the spirit out of the poor old bugger. Ragged-Trousered Philanthropist Tony Keth expressed exactly what wasn't on everyone's tongue when he said that the change in Jack from idiosyncratic working man to faceless service industry prole was what was happening to working people all over the country. Although, to be fair, he did have a point. But Jack worked on quietly, Penzance was getting its lights and people were happy on the whole. Sheila Mitchell's crisis was over.

The day before the opening ceremony, Jack put the finishing touches to the display, spending a remarkably long time arranging strings of lights over the entrance to the Market House at the top of Market Jew Street. Switching On Night would take place below its pillars and Jack laboured to make the very best of this important focal point, working quietly, carefully, humbly, like the remodelled, less troublesome working man he was.

Switching On Night arrived. About time, too. It was December 15 and the streets of Penzance had spent quite enough time in the gloomy darkness of midwinter, thank you very much. Jack walked across the promenade in an unusually jovial mood. He was not dwarfed at all by the great, dark sky and infinite ocean. In fact, he was thinking that out there across the sea other working men were taking their own secular and unopiated comfort in that feeling of warmth towards one and all that was aroused among even non-believers, yes Jack had to admit it, at Christmas. He walked up Chapel Street, peering into the windows of public houses. A fat man raised his glass and grinned at a friend in a window seat. And didn't it seem as if he were raising his glass to Jack Tremenyans?

Chapel Street was busier at the top and by the time Jack reached Queen's Square he found himself part of a crowd heading towards Humphry Davy Statue under Market House. He felt a hand on his shoulder. Councillor Simons grinned at him.

'How about us getting up on the platform with the dignitaries?'

'Dignitaries?' said Jack. 'I'd never associate with that shower of shit. If you want dignity you'll find it among these good people.' Jack waved his arm to encompass a full complement of Penzance's diverse citizenry: shopkeepers, OAPs, mothers with children, working men, his arm swiftly moving on from the not insubstantial contingent of drunkards, dreadlocked cynics and cannabis smokers, that ever-increasing band of social abstainers who found no place in Jack's social system and who – bafflingly – would sneer at Jack just as soon as they would the true enemy.

'Suit yourself,' said Councillor Simons. 'I just thought you might like to enjoy the show from the best seat in the house.'

'I suppose it won't hurt this once,' said Jack, waving away a cloud of sticky cannabis smoke.

Councillor Simons led Jack to the platform. The pair climbed the steps and were greeted by an effervescent

Sheila Mitchell, the pinched meanness she took for social decorum spirited away on a froth of champagne bubbles. In fact she was disarmingly flirtatious.

'And here he is,' she said, taking Jack by the hand and almost pulling him up the final step of the platform. 'The man who made all of this possible. I can't thank you enough, Mr Tremenyans.'

Sheila smiled and stared into his eyes with the fleeting earnestness of the intoxicated, her head slightly to one side as if studying the ruddy, simple goodness of the indigenous working man.

'Not at all, Mrs… Mayor Mitchell,' said Jack.

Sheila took his other hand in hers. They stood face to face now, like two old lovers renewing their vows.

'I shall have a thing or two to say about you in my speech, Mr Tremenyans.'

'That really isn't necessary,' said Jack.

'I insist. You are the star of the show. And the people of Penzance shall know it, too.'

The crowd was ready. The dignitaries were ready, fixed grins revealing nothing of the great battle at ground level, their feet inching forward as they jostled for space, cutting off glory routes from fellow councillors as they edged themselves towards the front of the stage and into the public gaze. Jack felt a pain in his toe. He looked down. A shiny black shoe was crushing his foot. Terry Maddern stepped in front of him, grazing the old socialist's shoulder as he came through. He grinned at Jack and mouthed 'sorry', then continued his journey forward on the stepping stones of fellow Tory toes until he was right at the front next to Sheila.

The crowd became impatient for the speech; or rather impatient for the conclusion of the speech so they could see the lights and get to the pub or go home.

A microphone squealed. The crowd fell silent.

'Wonderful,' said Sheila, her cool, half smile back again now. 'So very marvellous to see you all here this evening. It's on nights like tonight that we get the opportunity to acknowledge individual townsfolk for their hard work in bringing a little light to the community. Thank you, Sandra Hardman and the rest of the Lights Committee for raising money towards the new displays – and several hundred new bulbs – this year.'

A ripple of applause.

'Thank you to the Highways Committee for overseeing temporary diversions while the lights were hung.'

More applause, a little less enthusiastic this time, the Highways Committee an abstraction that failed to bring hands together with any real vigour.

'Thank you Toolkit Construction for assembling tonight's podium free of charge.'

Was that a clap or a smacked arse? In any case the crowd seemed to be losing interest.

'And finally while I shamefully, but I'm afraid unavoidably, implicate myself in this tribute, thank you to those members of the council who worked tirelessly in coordinating all the groups and individuals involved in bringing us what will, I'm sure, be a glorious display.'

Sheila paused and smiled demurely.

'What about Jack?'

'Yes, we want a bit of Jack.'

Gradually, a chant rose up from the crowd.

'We want Jack. We want Jack. We want Jack.'

Had Sheila forgotten? Perhaps, but she would certainly be reminded now. And yet still there was no room for Jack in her speech.

'And now the moment you've all been waiting for.' Sheila raised her arms. 'Best wishes, Penzance. And a happy Yuletide to one and all.'

Sheila pointed a finger in the air and dropped it onto a bright red button. A whooshing sound filled the air. Then, gradually, Penzance flickered to life, lights blinking here and there, fluttering like eyelids fighting for freedom from a long dark sleep before bursting into bright-eyed consciousness.

The crowd clapped and cheered. The councillors on the podium warmly applauded themselves. It was Christmas in Penzance at last and the festive spirit was with one and all.

Soon, too soon, the clapping and cheering from the crowd died away. The muffled sound of soft leather claps continued from the podium for a moment until the councillors, confused by the crowd's silence, fell silent too.

First came a titter. Next a snort. Then a few infectious chuckles from Ding Dong Williams that spread in all directions and grew into a ragged mess of hilarity. Some hooted, shaking and shaking, then doubling over, resting hands on knees as they gasped to fill empty lungs. Some screeched, throwing back their heads like gulls on chimney pots. Others cried, their faces twisted in uncontrollable mirth, tears falling down their cheeks. One or two laughed so violently that the medium of sound, unable to do justice to their merriment, gave up, and nothing came from their lungs but a rush and hiss of air, though they made up for their vocal deficiencies with some admirable thrashing about and staggering.

Gradually, a few of these hooters, screechers, weepers and hissers pulled themselves together enough to lift weak, shaky arms and point above them to the Market House. The councillors, who of course faced the crowd, had not an inkling what this was all about, and watched the bawdy shenanigans of the proletariat below with confused grins. Sheila Mitchell was the first to follow the pointed fingers to the source of the amusement and turn around. And there it was, above her, both implicating her in the coarsity of a hopeless, degenerate people and reminding one and all of the real hero of the evening.

Penzance smiled from the top of the Market House in a curve of brightly coloured, oddly assorted lights. One light was missing, a cheeky proletariat cavity suggesting a class of people not accustomed to six month check-ups. The bulbs were arranged skilfully by a local hero into words that summed up the genuine warmth of spirit in a Penzance Christmas greeting; summed it up in a way the chilly formality of Sheila Mitchell's podium greetings never could.

The immortal words of Jack Tremenyans.

'Merry Fucking Christmas.'

one big echo of a much nicer place

'SOMETIMES WHEN it's very quiet I think I can hear things from a long time ago and not even things around the house but things that happened a long way away. Do you know what I mean?'

'Not really, Barbara, no,' said Diane.

But Barbara would not be deterred. Her voice was all thick and she was smiling.

'I've stood in the kitchen, my hands in a sinkful of water, and heard two old men talking over at Godrevy Lighthouse. All the ins and outs of their lives. Do you know what I mean?'

Diane blew into her tea and sent up a cloud of steam.

'No, dear, I can't honestly say I do.'

'When I'm outside, I think it might just be the wind in my ears.'

'I expect that's what it is.'

'But I hear it all indoors too, so it can't be that.'

Diane put down her steaming cup.

'That was a lovely cup of tea, Barbara, but I can't stop. I've got Derek's lager T-shirts in the tumble dryer and he'll have my guts for garters if I shrink them.'

And she was out the door in a second, and Barbara was left smiling to herself and listening for her voices.

She was a funny woman, Barbara Morethek. That's what everyone said. She was normal enough to be part of the everyday circle of chat and what have you, but she had this odd side to her. You didn't want to peer too deeply into her. And when her voice got all thick like that you were in trouble. She was forty but she could have been fifteen years older. Her hair and eyes were dark brown – almost black – but her face was washed of all colour and from her eyes to her chin it was all sloping curves. Great lines on her cheeks dropped either side of her mouth, and several lines about the mouth pulled it chinward so that, even when she smiled, at best there was a wistful quality to her expression and usually an outright victory for sadness.

Because she was a sad person. She thrived on sadness and misery and she suffered for nostalgia so much that any pleasant event began to gather a yellow veneer even before the image had been fully committed to memory.

Her world was full of echoes from when the kids were young. She would sniff a chipped mug and smell pineapple squash because that's what Stuart used to like after school. A shadow in a corner, the flick of a kettle switch, the sound of a car passing on the road – inexplicable things made her heart ache.

Her husband, Peter, he'd had it up to here with her. And he would jerk a rigid hand to his chin when he said this to the boys down the pub, which he frequently did. 'Every fucking dinner is like the last supper,' he would say. 'I can honestly say, when she first got like this – two or three years in – I would open the door and see her and think: Christ Almighty, someone's died. I did. God's truth. And I'd say, "What's the matter, love?" And she'd say, "Nothing." Then she'd say, "Everything." Well is it one or the other? "Both," she'd say. Well, I ask you. What in God's name are you meant to do with a statement like that?'

He was a practical man, Peter, with a neat moustache. And if a statement contradicted itself, or was enigmatic or paradoxical, he was done with it. And quite often with the person who made it. Peter told everyone about Barbara, anyone who would listen. It made her a kind of comedy figure around town. And if she felt as if she watched the world through glass it was just as well, because many people saw her as an exhibit of sorts.

As a result Barbara wasn't a big fan of shopping. When she walked down Station Hill and turned into Foundry Square, things got big and echoey. It was hard to describe: it was as if she heard people's voices and made a memory of them at exactly the same time. And the sound of buses pulling away, the flash of a yellow mac, the smell of bread in the baker's: all were made to resemble the appearance, smell or sound of these things, but they weren't really these things at all. It was as if everything that is here has been borrowed for a day from somewhere else and it doesn't quite fit and anyway it will have to be returned soon to its proper place. Do you know what I mean?

But nobody knew what she meant.

There was one thing about shopping she liked, and that was buying her fruit and veg from Charles Spycer. Charles was a fat chap with a big, black beard who had a grocer's shack just off Foundry Square. He had great forearms covered in black hair and hands that looked like they could squeeze the life out of a plum or a satsuma. But he had a lovely deft touch with the fruit and veg and Barbara wasn't the only woman to notice it.

It wasn't just his hairy and imposing presence, however, that made Charles popular with the ladies; it was his easy manner and humour, too. His sense of fun, in fact, had such an influence it spilled into neighbouring territory, his great laugh drifting across slate-grey skies to threaten the misanthropy and torpor that Old Bastards Dick Elliot and Arthur Tredinnick cast over their corner of the square. And if he had a coarse turn of phrase – he never failed to delight in fruit-related crudity – his smile and his laugh tempered even the most outrageous obscenity.

'Hey, you watch what your Jack does with that when he gets home,' he'd say to Mrs Davies, pointing at a cucumber poking out of her bag. Then he would roar with laughter. Mrs Davies, genuinely affronted for a split second, would be swept away by his roar and wave him away with tears in her eyes, still feeling the reverberations of his and her own laughter half way up Foundry Hill.

'Hey, I swear blind,' he said to Barry Truscott one day. 'Stick a few of they grapes up your arse and fart and you'll never feel anything like it.'

And Barry, a quiet churchgoing man who liked a bit of fun, would stand rooted to the spot in front of Charles, weeping as he held straining bags by his sides, often holding up customers while Charles, relentless, whispered a few more fruit nothings into his ears.

Now Barbara had heard Charles in full flow and she found him funny like everyone else did. And the sound of his laughter seemed to be the only thing that made cracks in the glass jar she inhabited, and let a little air in. But it was more than his sense of fun. There was something about Charles that others didn't see. It was hard to describe. She saw it in his reflection in the scales while he weighed up her veg, or sometimes while he bent over to pick produce out from a crate at his feet. Barbara didn't know quite what it was at first, but she began to loiter over the road in the car park and watch Charles. And when Hayle was quiet, she discovered more of that thing others didn't see. He often stood in his shack, his hands behind his back and his lidded eyes staring at the fruit-stained floor. Sometimes his beard would start to move about in an odd, circular rhythm, too, as if he were gnawing away at his bottom lip.

On one occasion, Barbara saw something that made her heart leap. Standing in front of his shack, Charles spotted a stray plum by his foot. He reached down to pick it up, but changed his mind. Instead he looked left and right, and then lowered a great hiking boot onto that plum and squashed it into the ground, turning his foot back and forth over it to make sure it was dead. Barbara felt a strange joy. And, in a moment of poetry, she decided that Charles hid behind all the colours of his fruit, all the joy of oranges and plums, to disguise his sadness.

The next day she walked down Station Hill intent on making contact, hardly aware of the bland, pink faces that passed her. When she reached Charles's shack he bowed and waved her in, joking that he had some lovely prunes for her Peter's constipation. Barbara laughed.

When he turned his back to weigh some spring onions, she said: 'Sometimes, Charles, I feel as if I can hear people from long ago chatting away and they sound so happy they make me sad because I know I'll never meet them and to be honest when I hear them I feel as if there's no point to anything that's happening today and I might as well stay in bed. Do you know what I mean?'

Charles dropped the spring onions into the metallic weighing bowl and eyed her through the reflective casing of the machine.

'Yes, Barbara,' he said. 'I know exactly what you mean.'

***

They took walks together on the Towans and the beach. Refugees from happiness.
Often they sat beneath a dune with a rug covering their legs, looking out to sea.

'Sometimes I feel sad to think that the ripples on the sand will be gone later. And that no one but us will have seen them. Moments in time all wasted because people don't come to look at them. And they'll look at the sea where that sand was and say, "Oh, the sea's looking nice," and this and that, but they won't know about that bit of sand in that moment of time, will they, Charles?'

'I know. I'm terrible on trains,' said Charles, shaking his big head. 'Makes my heart break to see all those verges and sidings. And roundabouts, too, when you drive your car. To think there are lively town squares and shopping centres and what have you, and our homes – and then there are these little places that no one cares about or feels sad about except me.'

'I feel sad about them, Charles.'

He squeezed her.

'That's right. You do, too.'

Then they would walk on the sand when it was getting dark, down by the Hayle River, watching the swirl of river and sea in the glint of the sun as the curlews cried on the estuary and church bells from Lelant clanged in the distance.

'When I hear noises together like that,' said Barbara one day, 'I think to myself: They were meant to happen like that because something is talking to us. And it makes me sad to think we don't know what it's saying, because it might be able to tell us something that would help. Sometimes I think I'd rather not hear those noises at all than hear them and not understand. Do you know what I mean, Charles?'

'I know exactly what you mean. Beautiful things make me feel lonely.'

'The air this time of night is so still.'

'And the little bubbling sounds of the sand as the sea washes over.'

'Those pink clouds are like paintings, aren't they?'

'But they'll be gone in a minute.'

And so Barbara and Charles built an exquisite labyrinth of despair on Hayle beach, observing and cataloguing the sadness that is at the heart of animate and inanimate things: shells, seaweed, driftwood, old plastic bottles, thick bursts of marram grass, receding marram grass, the flashes of Godrevy Lighthouse, the darkness between the flashes of Godrevy Lighthouse, the sound of seagulls (a favourite of Charles's), the briny smell of salt in the air (a favourite of Barbara's), unknown footprints, their own footprints, the pattern of a few grains of sand on a finger, the three miles of sand that bordered the bay like a golden cutlass in the sun.

'I am so sad,' she said.

'Me, too,' he said.

And they kissed and were happy.

**

Barbara had learned to keep her gloomy thoughts from Peter. They made him irritable and angry. So together they kept up a pretence of civility and even-temper that was, in fact, as crushing to Peter as it was to Barbara. Even he could see that life was charade enough without this elaborate performance at home where lines were well rehearsed before they were even spoken. But that wasn't to say Peter was ready to give up the performance, even if it did have the gloom of an end-of-season matinee about it. Give up? And where would he be then? He may as well let his moustache grow until he looked like a big fucking walrus, or rip his clothes off and run about in the rain howling. The thought led only to madness. Since her afternoons with Charles, however, Barbara was finding it hard to hide her throbbing sadness. And she delivered her lines during domestic performances with increasing ineptitude. Peter found himself prompting her, lest the show should falter and ghostly titters and laughter descended on the Morethek household.

'I love bacon and eggs, don't you, Babs?' said Peter, feeding a sunny yolk into his face, bits catching on his moustache.

'Yes,' said Barbara. 'But there's something about the crispy bits of egg left behind on a plate that make me feel…'

'You know, they're full of protein, eggs,' said Peter, interrupting her. 'And calcium and B vitamins, too. Very good for you, they say.' He lifted his knife and tapped the air. 'But they say two a week is enough. Any more and you might be getting a bit too much cholesterol.'

'I've heard that,' said Barbara. And they were back in a world of facts that stray, ghostly feelings could not haunt.

And who was the audience at this faltering production now in its nineteenth year? The abyss, presumably, though ironically Peter wasn't one for drama when it came to words. But as the production began to falter and the cast looked increasingly tired, it was surely the abyss that began to heckle from the stalls, while Peter sweated under the heat and dazzle of the footlights.

***

It was close to Easter and the beach was getting busier. People walked their dogs and kids flew kites, and Barbara and Charles's melancholy landscape was infected with joy. They avoided people, partly because it was compromising for Barbara to be seen with Charles, but more because they were conscious of their own glum faces. When they did see people they forced smiles, which made their cheeks ache in the cold wind afterwards.

'Wouldn't it be nice, Charles, if we could be exactly as we are now all the time?'

They were hidden in the dunes away from the wind and prying eyes, huddled up next to a little window in the marram grass that looked over the sea towards St Ives.

Charles thought for a minute and bit into his big, black beard.

'Yes,' he said. 'Yes it would.'

A seagull flapped and came to rest in their little hollow. It looked at them with cold eyes.

'You,' said Charles, shouting at the seagull. 'Go and tell the people of Hayle that Charles Spycer is not a happy man. Tell them he's a miserable bastard who can't see the point of anything at all.'

The seagull cocked its head.

'And tell them that Barbara Morethek thinks the whole world is one big echo of a much nicer place,' said Barbara. 'And that I would rather have a day in the real world than a whole lifetime in this terrible land.'

The seagull backed off a couple of paces. It watched them. It chattered. Then, with a great flapping effort, it launched itself into the air, caught a gust and skidded away over the dunes, screeching. Barbara and Charles watched as it headed up the river towards the town.

'Listen,' said Barbara. 'It's telling them.'

They listened in silence until the cry of the seagull was lost in the cry of other gulls.

'He's telling them, but nobody's listening,' said Charles. 'They're all telling them, all those seagulls, about the sad and the lonely and the miserable, but nobody's listening.'

Bitter, beautiful words to Barbara's ears. Their time together had a sweet ache about it, like those moments after finishing a favourite book or poem. It was so wonderful to be sad with another, to feel their despair mingle with yours. Barbara wasn't sure if she ever wanted to be happy.

'There's only one thing for it,' said Charles. 'If they won't listen to the birds, we'll make them listen to us.'

***

Mr William Tresize bounced off the pavement and into Charles's shack. 'Charles, my lover, I'll have a pound of they purple plums.'

He looked at Charles with some expectation. After all, he'd fed him a gift of a line. But Charles lumbered about the shack like a man distracted, his big shoulders rounded and his head forward as if it threatened to roll off. Charles picked the plums one by one and slowly put them in a bag.

'Everything all right, Charles?'

'Not really.'

William smiled and shifted from foot to foot.

'Takings down are they?'

'They're up.'

Charles lumbered over towards the scales.

'Well, what is it?'

Charles turned to face William. He looked down into his black beard. 'I don't like plums,' he said. 'They depress me.'

William, a quick-featured chap, flicked his eyes here and there and grinned.

'He's a card,' he said.

Charles stood before him, plums swinging in a bag in his outstretched hand. William took the plums. He backed off slowly. 'He's a card,' he said again, and set off towards Foundry Square. He looked back. Charles stood in silence, his head down; overcome by plums. William felt the fruit swinging in his hand. 'I love a plum,' he said. 'That Charles is a card. And I do dearly love a plum.' And he took one more look back at Charles, who was now clearing away some boxes with a Sisyphean air.

These were early days, sketches; the show proper was yet to come. But that week Charles told Grace Pellow that bananas made him think of disease, Tommy Wakfer that there was something rotten-looking about pears even before they were ripe and Barry Truscott that aubergines made him think of death. Only Barry responded with anything like understanding. He nodded and said well, yes, aubergines were a very dark fruit, but it might help to see the purple rather than the black.

It was thoughtful and kind of Barry, but this was Charles being honest, himself: a miserable bastard who didn't want to try to be happy any more.

People were confused at first. Many suspected this was the beginnings of a new routine. That the humour in it all would become clear soon enough. But the carnival was over. The happy shack, where Charles had performed his sideshow attraction, glorying in the crudity of fruit, was gone. Now it was a theatre of despair, a one-man show that confronted a world of pain in relentless monologues, where customers found their fragile, brittle existences exposed during an innocent errand for fresh produce. It was a difficult show, what reviewers might refer to kindly as experimental. It was a Hamlet that was all soliloquy, a tragedy without a Rosencrantz and Guildenstern or Polonius. Charles held up turnips like Yorick heads. Back at home, customers stirred soups and stews with a melancholy slowness, as if the odours steaming up from Charles's veg infected their kitchens with sadness and decay.

Fewer and fewer customers came. And Charles stood sheltering from the rain in his shack as the trains thundered over the square. Mostly alone. Mostly thinking about sad things, or about Barbara and her sad things. Delighting in the sound of raindrops falling off his awning after a shower, or the shuffle of a beleaguered old dear puffing by on worn-out limbs. He had never felt so free before, so true to himself.

***

'Peter, I've got something to tell you.'

'Yes, Babs?'

'Peter, put down the remote and listen to me.'

'Don't be ridiculous, Babs. I'm watching the news.'

'I hate your moustache.'

'What?'

'Your moustache depresses me. When I look at it I think of DIY shops and men looking at pornographic magazines and corned beef and sentences like, "Plenty of salt and vinegar on that please, love," and, "Don't do anything I wouldn't do."'

'What the hell are you talking about. I'm trying to watch the news.'

Peter turned up the TV.

Barbara's eyes were shining. She leaned forward and spoke in a voice that was wounded but strong, too.

'Sometimes I think this life is a dream that's perhaps only a second long and I'm not really living in this house with you and you don't exist. And those voices over at the lighthouse are my friends trying to wake me up.'

Peter turned up the TV even louder. Barbara began to shout.

'Sometimes I think those funny little sounds in my head – those sounds and shadows and feelings that I can't explain – are more real than you are.'

The television was booming, vibrating. Barbara got up and shouted at the moustached head.

'I think there is nothing more unreal than this life we are living together.'

She snatched the remote from Peter's hand and turned off the TV. He continued to watch, feigning interest in the blank screen.

'Have you heard what I've said?' Barbara leaned in close and shouted at his head, as if Peter were an imbecile. 'I have just said the cleverest thing I'll ever say.'

It was impossible to ignore. Peter turned to her and began to speak. But nothing came. This wasn't right. This was out of his emotional range, his repertoire. He was the classically trained actor taking part in a nineteen-year run, suddenly confronted with renegade spontaneity in the female lead. He only had his old lines.

'I think I'll have a bacon sandwich for tea,' he said. 'Have we got any brown sauce?'

'Brown sauce reminds me of corduroy trousers and the Seventies,' said Barbara. 'I hate it.' And she threw back her head and laughed.

'What about a bit of pickle? I think I'll have a nice bit of pickle.'

'In white bread I suppose?' She thrust her fist at him. 'Why don't you have a nice bit of pickle in white bread and I'll tell you how pickle and white bread make me think of musty walk-in pantries and the smell of old people when they can't look after themselves any more. That would be nice, wouldn't it?'

Nothing made sense to Peter. The old order had been overturned in a moment. His sanity was now a form of insanity; her insanity sanity. He was addressing the abyss in the modulated tones of a man who believes there is order and truth beyond reason, and not madness; as if reason was not merely a convenience that kept you quiet until the panic of final understanding. He saw that the universe was with her, the insane, and not with him, the sane. He was being laughed at and heckled and booed off stage, but still he continued.

'It's okay,' he said. 'I understand.'

Barbara paused for breath. She was flushed and panting. 'You do?'

'We shall have a nice cod and chips.'

Again, Barbara threw her head back and laughed. It was unnatural to see her like this, so alive, so powerful, bending, swaying, pointing. It was the performance of a lifetime. And she continued to laugh at cod and chips and Peter watched her as she laughed and then a terrible thing happened to him: he began to smile. He grinned at her and his moustache tickled his nostrils. And she was looking at him with her head thrown back, perspective pushing her nose towards her eyes, flattening her face into a smaller two-dimensional space. And this was funny to Peter and he pointed at her and began to laugh himself. And the laughter grew and grew until it was apparent to Peter that it didn't emanate from him, it was a great rhythm entering him and shaking him like a doll. And he continued to laugh and point and the tears streamed down his eyes until he couldn't remember what he was laughing at; all he knew was that his mind and his emotions had broken free of their moorings and he didn't quite know where he was.

Barbara watched, fascinated.

'Wooh,' he went, as if he were on a scary ride. He giggled at her. 'Wooh.' He giggled again. And the man she hadn't loved for 17 years was breaking up in front of the woman he hadn't loved for 17 years. He started shaking his head and crying, but he still had time for the odd 'wooh' and burst of laughter as he plummeted towards the abyss. 'Wooh.'

It made her feel quite sad. It was exhilarating.

***

Barbara left Peter and moved in with Charles. They worked the stall together. Quiet, they were. Things settled down a bit for Charles: while he didn't revert to the fruit obscenities of yore or try to entertain his customers, he didn't force his misery on them quite so much either.

The pair of them worked the stall with slowness, with sadness, and the shack became a world of gloomy curios just as the Towans and the beach had in early spring. They held hands and listened to the flap of the wind through the canvas roof; they stared out at the dead hour of the afternoon – usually between two and three – when the world gave up the charade and surrendered to the silence; and they caught each other's eyes during the futile whitterings of a local radio talk show, which more than anything else suggested all the people here were exiled and the real world was somewhere far away.

People came back. Some of them. And those that didn't were replaced by a new breed. The shack became a beacon to the sad and the dispossessed. The miserable and the misanthropic came for their weekly shop and were spared the terrible effort of smiles and small talk, things which left them exhausted. The enthusiastically depressed came in and shook their heads slowly at the ways of the world, and the obsessives were allowed to check and rehearse their safety charms and spells without interruption. Even the less committed, the occasionally depressed – those who often took a cheerful morning to do half an hour's shopping because of endless little chance sociable meetings – even they visited the shack on those days when a brittle vulnerability came over them, when they would cross the street to avoid even a close friend.

Barbara had seen Peter. It took him a while to get over the shock, but he seemed to have come out the other side. He was on the sick and he'd lost quite a few clients, but he was giving up plumbing anyway. He smiled a lot when he talked and he'd grown a beard. He talked fast. In fact he'd speeded up all over, as if he were making up for lost time. He said he had only one plan: to sell ice-creams on Hayle beach in the summer. He had a vision, he said, of walking across the warm sand barefoot with a cooler on his shoulder and seeing kids' faces light up when he called out, 'Aiiiice cream!'

Barbara was glad she'd left him.

Some people said it was all her fault, that she'd ruined Charles and Peter. Barry Truscott thought differently. He said she'd been the making of them both.

Everything had changed. Barbara even looked different. The lines on her face – no they didn't fade, they deepened; they became more etched in her face, more of her face, rather than the enemy of her features.

'I love you, Charles,' she said, one day.

'I love you, too,' he said.

And they listened to car tyres hissing through the wet after a shower, they listened to the drips on the awning and the seagulls squawking and shaking their feathers on the roofs and they were miserable. Wonderfully, wonderfully miserable.

richer than the kingdom of heaven

YOU YOUNGSTERS you sit around and think about this and that and get your depression or your panic attacks but we had nothing like that in my day. When you get to my age you'll see that there is nothing to do with life but live it. We're all going to die, boy. We're all going to be dirt in the ground. So live it like you're in a panic. Love like you've got toothache. Go on the piss for a week. I did all that. And now I'm getting on I can sit and watch telly on a sunny evening without thinking, Christ, I should be out there enjoying a sunset, or what have you, because I did it all already and I'm knackered, boy. Absolutely worn out and done with it. And happy. You laugh at me for recording quiz shows and watching them two or three times, but you wouldn't laugh if you knew what I got up to in my time.

I've got some stories I could tell you. I only have to look out the window for the past to come alive again. See Marjorie Carne walking along the terrace. Christ, she's gone to seed. We all have. I had her in the cellar of the Cornish Arms one New Year's Eve, only the barrel we were leaning on went over and beer shot up out through the pumps upstairs. When we came up Derek English said, 'I'll have what Tommy's having.' They still call a pint of mild a pint of Marjorie up the Cornish Arms. And that's just Marjorie and she just happened to be walking by.

But I could tell you a story like that about half of these old souls coming up and down the terrace. I know what you're thinking, because I thought the same at your age. It's hard to imagine these shrivelled-up old dears were once full of life and smiles and beauty, but they were, boy.

Be thankful for what you've got. All those young girls running around after you for no other reason than you're young. And you running around after them for the same reasons. But, before you know it, all that long hair they toss about will be drying out and the perfume they wear will get stronger and they'll be wearing trinkets and what have you and carrying silly little bags with this and that in them because they aren't girls any more they're ageing old birds.

And you'll be an ageing old bastard, too. And that's all right. For them and for you. There's no use moaning about it. And you won't moan about it as long as you have nothing to regret. Squeeze the life out of it. Squeeze every moment till your face is like a bloody beetroot. That's what I did.

Talking about bastards, see Arthur Tredinnick there outside the bakery? Now, I know what you think about Arthur. Standing outside the bakery every day with Dick Elliot, looking miserable. But Arthur was a great comedian in his day. And a practical joker. We were famous friends back then. One Bonfire Night – this is when we were kids – we were letting off bangers all over the place. A policeman came up Tremeadow Terrace and said to Arthur, 'Now, young Master Tredinnick, do you know anything about fireworks being let off up and down the terrace.' And Arthur said no he didn't but he would keep his ears open. Well, the policeman walked on and Arthur crept up right behind him, lit a banger, threw it between his legs and ran like hell. Well, my Christ Almighty, I've never seen anything like it. Eric Firth – that was the copper's name – he must have jumped three feet in the air. Me and Arthur made it up to the old rope works and hid away. Arthur was crying and moaning so hard – the tears coming down his face, clutching his hands to his stomach like this – I thought he'd lost a finger in the blast. But he was laughing, laughing so hard he could hardly breathe. And that's just one story about me and Arthur and there's hundreds more.

That's what you've got to remember. Every new lot that comes up thinks they invented shenanigans, boozing and fighting. Us older ones smile to each other when we see that. Christ, my Uncle Sandy would come home from the pub with blood all over his hands. He was a hard bastard. Forget your Clint Morris. Uncle Sandy would have hammered him with one hand and kept his pint steady in the other.

The problem with you kids is that you think this town popped into existence just when you knew your arses from your elbows. But there was some loving and laughter and tragedy before you were even thought of. Did you know that fifty year ago Hayle was full of Americans? Or that the beach was mined in the war? Or that Malcolm Perkins' brother got tangled in weeds and drowned in Copperhouse Pool while we all watched and we tried to get to him but we couldn't and by the time Bill reached him he was dead? I expect you've never even heard of Titty Perkins. He had the biggest ears I've ever seen.

Now, see that Roger Chivell by Spar. Sour before his time he is. A miserable bastard. I knew his father Jeffery and he saw it coming. I expect you've never heard what happened have you? About his crowd over in St Ives. Some bastard came down from Kent way. Hippy. Late Sixties it was. Fell in with Roger and his girlfriend, Rosie. They were breathing in and breathing out. All the Buddhism and meditation nonsense. That was when the mellow yellow chap lived in St Ives. What was he called? Anyway, Roger lapped it up and grew his hair. There was a whole crowd of them like that over St Ives. Roger told Jeffery that everything is pretend and the world is an illusion. He gave up boozing, too. Jeffery couldn't stand it no more. Well, he said to Roger, illusion or no, I'll tell you something real. That hippy is getting too friendly with your Rosie for my liking. Roger laughed at him and told him to mind his own business. But Roger caught them one day. They thought he was out but he was in his bedroom concentrating on his breathing. And that hippy – who was an expert on not following his cock apparently and on giving up everything that brings a bit of pleasure to life – well, he was giving Rosie one on the kitchen table. And poor old Roger in the bedroom wasn't concentrating on his breathing any more he was concentrating on their breathing, because they were at it like rabbits.

Roger kicked the shit out of the boy but he still married Rosie. Jeffery said he still believed everything was an illusion, but he didn't seem so happy about it any more. That's gospel truth.

And I know you think I'm too old to understand, but I know about all that crowd with their incense and their India. Keep clear of that lot. Cornwall is crawling with them. Tell them to shove their horoscopes and their cards and their breathing up their arses. They love all these quoits and witches and crosses but they're not interested in what a real Cornishman thinks. Too much fucking and farting. Stay away from them. Stay away from po-faced bastards who hate to admit we're made of flesh and blood. Who want to empty their minds. I tell you fill your mind up, boy. One thing I can't stand is people who think they're too good for flesh and blood. We are flesh and blood, for Christ's sake. First we're young flesh and blood, then we're old flesh and blood and then we're rotting flesh and blood and then we're nothing. I smile at that. You'll understand one day. And those bastards – they think they're going to live forever and they look so fucking miserable about it.

They're miserable because they treat this world like a waiting room when it's rich boy, richer than the kingdom of heaven. Even Hayle. Especially Hayle.

clink clink clink

'PLEASE, GOD, let Marjorie Eddie be late, ill or dead,' thought Florence Bray as she waited at the bus stop. 'Because if I have to spend today of all days on a coach with that woman, I will slit my throat.'

And Florence giggled to herself at her wickedness. She had known Marjorie for fifty years; they were best friends. And yet she couldn't stand the woman.

The old bus shuddered over the bridge and pulled up next to Florence, coughing smoke not unlike the late Woodbine Evans. Florence kept her eyes down. The sight of old people looking from buses depressed her. They gazed jealously at the small vignettes of life passing them by, craning their necks as if forever departing. Florence never imagined she'd step on one of these buses. But she did now. Most Thursdays.

Just like Marjorie.

'Florence! How lovely,' said Marjorie, calling from the back of the coach. And the silly woman, with her silly red lipstick and her big thick glasses smiled as if Florence were the best thing in the world.

Florence smiled back: when you are old you must learn to smile at every annoyance and indignity if you are to survive the day, of course. She walked past Mr Drew, Elise Morgan and one or two others who still had some sense about them, and sat next to Marjorie.

'A trip to Fowey! Isn't it lovely, Florence?'

'I suppose it is,' said Florence, as she sat down. 'If you like Fowey.'

Marjorie grinned and pushed her face too close to Florence's. 'But you love Fowey. You and Stanley used to have your special trips there when you were younger.'

'Yes, dear, but that was then and this is now. And Stanley is gone and Fowey is not the Fowey of 1958.'

Marjorie popped a rhubarb and custard into her mouth, hunched her shoulders and grinned. She took abuse from Florence with impeccable good humour.

Florence was disappointed with herself for reacting so harshly. Disappointments were not unusual. She had lived a life of them. And yet she made a point of not looking back on life's bitter journey – at the regrets and the might-have-beens – but rather looking forward and searching quite enthusiastically for new things to be disappointed in. She had no time for Marjorie's mawkish sentimentality.

Yet Marjorie, as always, was relentless.

'Of course, your Stanley would have dearly loved a bit of trip like this, wouldn't he Florence? Remember the day when Eric Polkinghorne – grand Mr Eric Polkinghorne – drove me, you, Stanley and my brother Donald all the way to St Ives in his Bentley.'

'Yes, dear,' said Florence.

'On the back roads to St Ives, the sun shining, the golden gorse. Do you remember how your Stanley said the gorse smelled like coconut and Mr Polkinghorne – and he should know – said your Stanley had something of the poet about him?'

'Yes, dear.'

And Marjorie heaped up the past like shovelsful of earth. And today it threatened to bury Florence.

They passed Hayle on the bypass.

'Now look at that,' said Florence. 'Those plans for five hundred homes, a marina and goodness knows what else haven't come to much. Hayle is a dump and it always will be.'

And she felt relieved to be talking about real things,

things you could see and not murky moments from days long gone.

'Of course,' said Marjorie, 'they first started on about a marina in Hayle as far back as 1964! I remember because Derek said…'

Florence stared at the head-rest in front of her. She took a deep breath and stood up.

'I'm awfully sorry, Marjorie, but I promised dear old Mr Drew I would sit with him a while.'

And before Marjorie had time to answer, Florence made her escape, sidling down the aisle and dropping into the seat next to the old man. And if she'd done a mean thing by leaving Marjorie, she'd done a good thing by joining Mr Drew. No one else would sit next to him anymore.

'I hear you upset a few people on the trip to Padstow, Mr Drew,' she said. 'I demand to know the reason why. God knows I've tried but I can't get it out of Marjorie.'

Mr Drew stared out of the window. Eventually he turned to face her. 'It will come to nothing, of course,' he said, ignoring her question.

'What will?' said Florence.

'This trip.' Mr Drew licked his white moustache and fiddled with his thick black glasses. 'We shall be tipped out the coach at Fowey and have our chips stolen by gulls. Then we shall be back on the coach with no stops on the way home, and all desperate to urinate before we reach even Camborne.' Mr Drew turned to Florence. His old eyes glittered. 'And what do you think of that, woman?'

Florence thought it was marvellous. She turned to get a good look at the old man. He had a headful of thick white hair, yet there was nothing benign about the old duffer. In fact, from Camborne to Redruth he licked his lips, fiddled with his glasses and made dark, apocalyptic pronouncements about the plight of the elderly so rhythmic and relentless one could hear the beat of the approaching Four Horsemen in his delivery.

'We shall all go, my dear,' he said. 'We shall all go alone in the end. And not all peacefully either.'

And that moustache never got so good a licking, or the glasses a fiddling as when he waxed lyrical on the final moments. He never seemed so alive in this autumn of his life as when looking towards chill winter.

The bus stopped for coffee just outside Truro. It was one of those dreadful cafes sat in a glorified layby, a bleak interzone where old dears on coach trips are fed and watered as the rest of the world rushes by without a second glance. Florence entered reluctantly. Orphaned things littered the cafe, things that might have been collected from the side of the road over decades: several mottled Elvis mirrors on a sticky pine wall; saucy postcards, so British and so sad; a silver trophy, looking lonely and defeated at one end of a high empty shelf; and a middle-aged man in denim with long, thin hair balding at the crown.

She found a table and sat down with Mr Drew. Marjorie sat at the next table playing cards with a few sour church cronies. Florence cheered up – she would certainly not be invited. Mr Drew licked his lips and spoke of the dreadfulness of his coffee. The bus driver stood outside, staring into space and smoking away his time. Marjorie glanced over to Florence occasionally. She caught Florence's eye and grinned as if she were having the most marvellous time in the world.

'I know something you don't,' she said, calling across to Florence.

'What's that then, dear?'

'You don't remember, do you?'

Florence looked at Mr Drew and turned up her eyes.

'You and your Stanley stopped here on your way back from Llandudno. I remember because you remarked on the pig dressed as a chef on the menu board. And you said…' Marjorie glanced at the ladies around her, a sheepish look on her face but also a sparkle in her big eyes.

'I said the food wasn't fit for pigs,' said Florence.

'That's it!' said Marjorie, her shiny clown's lipstick spreading across her face. 'And I never did forget it.'

'You didn't, did you,' said Florence. Of all days, she thought, not today. But it was too late. This cafe, this rubbish dump of forgotten objects and faded memories, began to fill with Stanley, morose Stanley, who drank his dishwater coffee with reluctance as they sat in silence. And above them that chalk pig – yes, a chalk pig a splash of water could destroy – lived on though Stanley, a thing of flesh and blood, was gone. And so Marjorie heaped more earth on Florence, as if she would bury her out of spite for having a past when she herself had none. And yet the woman was too stupid to be malicious.

'And the other thing that reminded me about your stopping here was…'

'I'm awfully sorry, dear,' said Florence, interrupting. 'But Mr Drew was telling me all about his problem.' She looked at the old dears one by one. 'Nine days. And not a thing worth flushing.'

Rheumy eyes bored into cards. Even Marjorie seemed to forget Florence as she arranged and rearranged her seven cards. As for Mr Drew, he was licking his moustache and looking about him as if searching for errant boys bereft of school ties.

'Another cup of coffee, please,' he said, pointing at no one in particular, although perhaps to the pig on the board because he did gesticulate somewhat in that direction.

Florence got up, left the table and stepped outside. She had let her anger run away with her again, just like Stanley always said she did. And yet it had worked – she had washed away the past with something far more memorable than a pig on a return trip from Llandudno. And yet poor Mr Drew.

'Can I have one of those?'

She ponced a cigarette off the driver and they stood smoking together in silence, watching the cars whoosh by on the road. What has brought me here, outside Truro in a glorified layby on a spring day in 2008, thought Florence. And she thought about the past briefly, felt the essence of it in a moment. And not a moment more. The past was a thing upon which you stood firmly, it was the foundation that brought you here now – nothing more. And yet so many of those old dears immersed themselves in the past, they wallowed in it, their feet sunk in so far they could barely move in the present.

And yet I feel as if I have hardly started, thought Florence. She sucked her fag. And then she thought the thing it seems obscene to think when you are old: I wish I could live forever. And it was true: disappointed, bitter Florence would gratefully accept an eternity of bitter disappointments. What was the alternative?

Marjorie and her church friends walked out of the cafe. Marjorie grinned at Florence.

'On the other hand,' thought Florence, stubbing out her fag. 'There are a few things worse than death.' And she laughed out loud at her wickedness and got back on the bus.

***

Florence sat down next to Mr Drew. 'I'm dreadfully sorry,' she said. The old man stared straight ahead. 'I don't know what came over me.' Mr Drew fiddled with his glasses. The old tongue arced over the moustache. He turned to Florence.

'I know exactly what came over you. You reached your limit with that infernal woman.'

'Marjorie?'

'I have watched over the years, Mrs Bray, and I have seen something in your relationship that I have also observed in the relationships between my schoolboys.'

'What is it, Mr Drew?'

'She is a leech, and a pernicious influence on your character.'

'Surely not?'

'If you were boys, I would protect you from her by keeping each of you at opposite ends of the class.'

They sat in silence. The bus pulled away. Florence was confused. Mr Drew clearly had a bee in his bonnet about Marjorie and had gone too far. But for the very first time in her life, Florence did not feel guilty about the way she treated her. Mr Drew had defended Florence's actions. Stanley never had. Quite the opposite. He would shake his head at her harsh words about Marjorie, or anyone else for that matter, and walk away as if there was no saving her, nothing to be done but to retreat from her toxic influence.

'Thank you, Mr Drew,' said Florence.

'Thank me, woman?' Mr Drew turned away from her and looked at the passing countryside. 'I should thank you. You have some gumption, Mrs Bray, some passion and fire. And it is a wonderful thing to see a group of narrow-minded, churchgoing prigs scandalised, I can tell you. I would put up with all the constipation in the world for it.'

Mr Drew spent the remainder of the journey informing Florence of the ungodliness of modern churchgoers. And she was reminded once again that he was quite mad.

'I know the Bible like the back of my hand and I'll tell you this: these women in their pastel hats are devils, my dear. And they hide themselves by getting as close to God's earthly objects as possible.' He paused. 'I am talking churches, of course. Now, if I had my way I'd turf 'em out of church and chuck 'em down a well and into Hell. There's too much lip-service to God among the pastel fiends. Too much pinch-mouthed servitude and not enough love and devotion. They like nothing more than to frown or snipe at any of us old ones with a bit of fire left in our bellies.'

Mr Drew turned to Florence. 'They won't speak to me, Mrs Bray.'

'Why is that, Mr Drew?'

Mr Drew didn't reply. He was lost again, gazing into the middle distance and licking his moustache with relish; perhaps tasting sulphur on the bristles as he leaned over his well and dropped his pastel fiends into hellish torment.

They reached Fowey. Florence and Mr Drew got off the bus.

'A word of advice. Keep away from that woman.'

'But where are you going, Mr Drew?'

'You don't want to spend a pleasant spring day with a gloomy old man.' He waved her away. 'Now be off with you.'

And before Florence had time to tell him that she would have given anything to spend the day with a gloomy old man, he was striding down the car park and towards the harbour.

Florence was alone. Others were getting off the bus. She saw Marjorie grinning at her through the glass. She hurried off towards the harbour. And here she was again.

Fifty years to the day. Walking down these narrow streets.

Weeks ago she had seen the date of the trip and decided she would not come to Fowey. And yet she came, telling herself that new memories would obliterate the old. Through a narrow gap between houses, she saw a gleaming white cruise ship on the water. That's the life I would like, thought Florence. Always sailing away. Maybe she would go on a cruise.

She reached the harbour front, leaned on the railings and looked across towards Polruan. The sun warmed her. The water shimmered with light. Crisp voices cut through the still air. It was the beginning of spring, the bittersweet beginning of spring that reminds you of the possibilities to come, but also makes you turn about and see the long, darkness of a grey Cornish winter. Her Cornish winter had lasted fifty years. Florence wanted it all back. She wanted every second back so she could spend it: wisely this time. Stanley had been gone just three months, yet she saw so much differently already.

Seagulls screeched in the blue sky, piercing holes in time. Chatter and laughter. Chatter and laughter. She closed her eyes and felt the sun on her face. She saw the shifting red and black before her eyelids as puffs of cloud passed over the sun. She heard the swoosh of a wing close to her face. She was happy for a moment, living simultaneously in a time before and after Stanley. Who would have thought in Fowey, today, she could find moments like these? It was true: she had spirit, she was a formidable woman.

'Boo!'

Florence opened her eyes.

'I thought I might find you here.'

Florence turned around. Her vision slowly cleared of white and red. Marjorie materialised. Spinsterly, mousey

Marjorie. Grinning Marjorie, with flakes of that incongruous red lipstick lifting off her lips.

'Are you having a nice time?' she said.

'Lovely,' said Florence.

Marjorie joined her at the railings.

'What a happy life you've had, Florence.'

'Have I?'

'And to think it all started here in Fowey. On this very same day. And here we are now.'

Florence gripped the cold railing and looked out at the gleaming ship on the water.

'And you and Stanley sat on a bench by the harbour.'

Marjorie squeezed Florence's hand.

'Do you think it might be this bench?'

She scuttled away and sat down behind Florence.

'Please come and sit on your bench with me.'

Florence turned around. Marjorie sat very rigid.

'And the thrill, Florence, you must have felt when Stanley said, "Florence, I have something very important to say, but I shall need an ale before I am quite brave enough to say it."'

Florence turned back and watched the light bursting on the water. The light of a glorious spring day.

'And so you got up and walked to the Red Lion. You had a strawberry ice-cream in your hand, didn't you Florence, but the barman waved you in and smiled and you sat in one of those cosy little cubicles. And you were thrilled, thrilled from head to toe. And Stanley, poor nervous Stanley, he held your hand and his big blue eyes looked into yours and he pulled a ring out of his pocket and said, "Florence, my dear, I want to spend my life with you. Will you marry me."'

Marjorie was speaking strangely, carefully. Florence turned around.

'And there were tears in his eyes, weren't there

Florence? And his fingers trembled as you held out your hand for the ring and he dropped it and it rolled off the table and went clink clink clink as it bounced on the stone floor.'

'Stop it!'

Marjorie stopped. She grinned.

'Did I get something wrong?'

Her big eyes glittered.

'It went clink clink clink, but he picked it up,' she said. 'And then he put it on your finger.'

And Marjorie, in happy reverie at Florence's happy life, reached down to her handbag on the ground and began scrabbling around for a rhubarb and custard.

Florence stood over Marjorie. She wanted to say something vulgar, to abuse the woman, but she felt weakened, overwhelmed by her words. Even this anniversary, this day, which was the only really important day of her life with Stanley, Marjorie would not leave to Florence. And the way she had looked without truly looking, lost in her reverie as she was, and the little smile on her lips... she was not delighting in Florence's memories, she was living in them. More than Florence ever had.

Marjorie was still scrabbling in her bag. Florence walked away without a word. Then, when she was a few steps away from Marjorie, she began to hurry as fast as she could without running. She made her way through the narrow streets, weaving through tourists. And though the day was alive with the smell of garlic and fish from restaurants, the hurble burble of pub chatter, the cool of the shade and then the warmth of the sun on her skin, she felt overwhelmed by memory. The thought of Marjorie still so near made Florence go further and further until the crowds thinned out and she was finally alone. She stopped to sit on the steps of a church. She was in the shade. She had never been here with Stanley before. Or Marjorie for that matter. The granite felt cool on her behind. It was empty and quiet. A blackbird sang somewhere above. Florence relaxed. Marjorie and the past seemed far away. This is what she wanted for the remainder of her life: to feel the simple pleasures of today. She sat there for a long time, watching the precious minutes pass as the light grew thicker.

Clink clink clink.

Florence frowned. She closed her eyes and took a deep breath.

Clink clink clink.

Why did the thought of that ring dropping to the floor make her so angry? No, not the ring dropping. It was perhaps the sweetest moment as Stanley smiled awkwardly and reached for it, his chin touching the table as his hand pawed at the floor. When he sat up his chin was wet with beer. Florence wiped it with her handkerchief. It was an intimate moment; the finest moment before it all changed. A moment so rare, so delicate one does not put it into words.

Clink clink clink.

Florence frowned again. She had never put it into words. She had held it close to her heart all these years. And yet Marjorie knew. And the way she had spoken, the way it all came out at the harbour, it was clear she had held this precious moment close to her heart for years, too.

Something came over Florence, a terrible feeling that in a moment swallowed up the cold silence of fifty years and filled it with clammy warmth. She got up and walked back slowly through the narrow cobbled streets, towards Marjorie. It was busier than ever. Florence shuffled through the crowd. She thought about what prigs Marjorie and Stanley were. An awful thought occurred to her, a thought that made Marjorie, with her church and her values, seem both the saddest and the wickedest person she had known: she had introduced Stanley to Florence. And then she hadn't left their sides in fifty years. The past came alive to Florence in a fresh, new way. She thought of Marjorie's father. Of that stern Methodist with a good dose of snobbery thrown in. And of Stanley's father who poured his tea into his saucer and slurped it up noisily.

Florence reached the harbour front. Marjorie wasn't there. She sat on the bench – her bench – to think. Then she got up, held the railings and looked out on the water. She did not see things with the freedom and the clarity of earlier. She felt dazed, hazy. Nothing seemed quite real. She waited for Marjorie and then she realised Marjorie would not come. She thought of Marjorie's clink clink clink and then her clink clink clink and she knew exactly where to find her.

Florence walked back into the busy streets. She thought of a time and a place fifty years ago and a time and a place now, and she did not know what to expect of either, as if past and present were equally malleable, equally incomplete. She arrived at the Red Lion and looked in the window. And there was Marjorie, sitting at Florence's place with a soft drink. Her eyes darted around, greedily taking it all in, and a flaky red smile grew on her lips as she rubbed her finger over the grain of the wooden table.

And Florence felt the anger rise up in her as she thought of Marjorie's mousey act, her helplessness. She felt angry at how she had admired Stanley for feeling sorry for Marjorie, for urging Florence to invite Marjorie along to Sunday lunch or a trip to the cinema. She had responded enthusiastically – anything to fill the silence of their marriage. Florence thought about a life wasted, lives wasted, and the anger grew inside her. She stepped inside the pub and headed for Marjorie's table.

'Hello, Marjorie,' she said. 'I know all about you and Stanley.'

Marjorie looked up, startled, her magnified eyes growing as she apprehended a cold, formidable Florence.

'What do you mean?'

'You loved each other.'

'Sit down, Florence.'

'I prefer to stand.'

'But nothing happened between Stanley and me.' Marjorie frowned, as if scrutinising the past for any hint of indiscretion. 'Nothing at all.'

'I believe that, Marjorie, but I wish for all of our sakes it had.'

'What an awful thing to say,' said Marjorie. 'What a terrible thing to say.'

'I've come to say goodbye,' said Florence. 'I never want to see you again. Our paths shall cross at the Co-op or the chip shop, of course, but I shall say hello dear and you will too and we shall leave it at that.'

'But fifty years?' said Marjorie, her big eyes imploring Florence.

'And forty-five too long. I went off you a long time ago. But you are very difficult to get rid of.'

'Oh, what would Stanley think!'

'Do you know, I have absolutely no idea. You are a far better authority on the man than I am. Well, you are welcome to him now. And to all those marvellous memories. Enjoy them, Marjorie. Because I never did.'

***

Florence walked through the streets, heading for the harbour. Everything seemed utterly different, utterly new, as if she saw it as her life really was for the first time. And nothing more so than that day fifty years ago when Stanley slid the ring on her finger and they clasped hands. And they stayed that way for quite some time, feeling the warmth grow between each other's fingers.

And then, and Florence remembered it so vividly, it was time to do something else, to say something, to develop the moment, but all Stanley did was stare at the young men at the bar and grin at their jokes and laughter. And because Stanley was not looking at her, Florence looked too and they watched the comings and goings of the world as if they were not fully part of it any more, not part of anything, not even each other. And this precious, important moment of her life had something of the feeling of endings about it, of resignation, though she did not know why. And as she grew older she learned phrases like 'the thrill of the chase' and 'young love' and 'innocent youth' and she began to understand that what happened to her and Stanley that day is what happens to everyone.

We are all tricked by the myth of romantic love, the necessity of a myth that keeps the world turning. And she believed that other men and women felt just like her, that it was all a trick, and she only ever got a feeling that perhaps she felt it more than the others when she did something bad like cheat at cards. Because they had frowned at her as if it were a wicked thing to do. But Florence did not understand because it was only a game. It was all a game. But now in these moments – and the rush of these moments, the pounding of the blood in her head, the panic: my life, my God, all my life! – she felt she had made a dreadful mistake. She felt that the useless moments heaped up under her might have been precious ones, only she had squandered them because she had been tricked into believing that this life was nothing but

66

a cruel joke made up of one disappointment after another; into believing there is nothing to do but prepare oneself for the ultimate joke by drying up and slowly turning to stone so that towards the end one may begin to crumble quite painlessly and return to dust without any regrets at all.

***

'So, woman, soon we shall be back on our bus, shuddering away from Fowey and belching foul diesel as we go.'

'Not now, Mr Drew. I need to be alone.'

Mr Drew sat down. They looked at the cruise ship out in the harbour.

'I shan't pry, Mrs Bray. But if you would care to share your problem, God, in his infinite humour, has given me a remarkably large pair of ears with which to listen.'

Florence turned to look at Mr Drew's ears. And it was true – they were remarkably large.

'That's just it. This will sound very sentimental coming from a woman like me, but I've come to think of my entire life as some sort of joke.'

'This is marvellous.'

Florence moved away a little from Mr Drew. 'Why ever would you say such a thing?'

'Because you have joined the club at last. And I am delighted for you.' Mr Drew patted her knee. 'There are some – and those women in their pastel hats come to mind – who will never join us at all. And will take it all far too seriously.'

'I think you are talking generally, Mr Drew, while I have a specific situation in mind.'

'We all have our specific situation,' said Mr Drew,

licking his white moustache. 'Every last damned one of us. But some of us refuse to wake up to the truth. And yet the infirmities of age gives us every opportunity!' Mr Drew pointed at the ship. 'There, Mrs Bray, floats a small nation of elderly people, turning up their noses, keeping up appearances and scrabbling for the captain's table. I bet there is no more than a handful that see the marvellous opportunity for fun, once you get the joke, of course.'

'I see your point,' said Florence. 'But I think there are some of us who are more tricked than others.'

'I believe that is true,' said Mr Drew.

'Did you ever know anything about Marjorie Eddie? Anything I should know?'

'Only what I have told you. One must tread carefully around solicitous friends who are anxious to do everything for us, who put themselves below us. It is their intention to make us wicked so they might make themselves pure. Or at least appear pure.'

'Very profound, Mr Drew. You are quite the philosopher.'

'It is the duty of the old to philosophise,' said Mr Drew. 'And to laugh at themselves.'

'Such maxims!'

'I believe you are making fun of me. And that is good. None of us will cure all this heartache by being pious and miserable in a damned cold church.'

'So we come back to your pastel brigade.'

'The fiends!' said Mr Drew.

'Why don't they speak to you?' said Florence.

'Has it ever occurred to you, that God's jest was to shrink our bladders just in time for the age of interminable coach trips?'

Florence felt tired all of a sudden. And irritable. 'For God's sake, Mr Drew. What does all this mean?'

'Hush woman. You asked me why the devils don't speak to me and now I will tell you.' Mr Drew licked his lips. 'On a trip to Padstow, I drank two pints of ale. It was late in the afternoon and on the return journey I suffered an acute need to urinate. The driver, with all the intolerance of youth on his side, damn him, refused to leave the A30 and instead pulled into a lay-by.' Mr Drew turned to Florence. 'The tuts, Mrs Bray, as I walked down that aisle to relieve my pain! What godliness is there, I asked myself, in propriety? None, I thought. I was full of rage and thunder, Mrs Bray. And still a little drunk. Then, damn, it, I thought, I shall be godly and vulgar.'

Florence sat up straight and looked at the old man.

'What on earth did you do?'

'I stepped off the bus and walked a few paces towards the foliage. Then I turned towards the bus, pulled down my fly and pissed back at them.'

Florence gripped his arm. 'That is wonderful, Mr Drew.' And she felt the laughter rise within her and then escape and she hung on to mad old Mr Drew. She thought of Marjorie, the old dears on the bus, of Stanley, and she felt a stranger to them all now. Bitter tears fell with happy ones. Yet she felt relieved, as if she were getting rid of the tears, the people. When she finished, she looked out over the water glinting in the early evening light.

'We must go soon,' she said.

'Shall we have a drink first?' said Mr Drew.

'Have we time?'

Mr Drew looked at his watch. 'Plenty. Though we must drink shorts if we are to save our shrunken bladders.'

'Very wise,' said Florence.

She smiled and got up. She was being led astray by

a wicked, mad old man and it felt wonderful. It made her feel innocent and new. 'Lead on, Mr Drew,' she said. And as the old man led the way, Florence pulled the ring from her finger and threw it away. Clink clink clink, it went. And dropped into the water.

dandy allcock

HAYLE PEOPLE could tolerate Dandy Allcock in only very small doses. And while he did have something of the down-at-heel gameshow host about him, sweeping through the streets of the town in a flash of yellow teeth and bottlegreen jacket, his trousers brown – corduroy, of course – his eyes darting left and right, as flickering as his grin was steadfast, his arms waving around him so as to encompass the harbour and the vista out to St Ives, as if he were offering them as a prize in a tawdry television show… and while, yes, he did visit confused old dears in old peoples' homes and puckered his lips into outraged Os at some bit of sauciness from Mrs Clemens, checking his watch with a bent-arm flourish as he waved them goodbye and departed, leaving a sad, silent aura of faded celebrity that competed with the smell of stale urine for sheer afternoon bleakness… and while, also, he rushed through town (no one knew whither) nodding at acquaintances and strangers alike with an air of obligation, for to leave anyone out would create resentment among townsfolk who craved his attention… while Dandy Allcock was this overwhelming montage of irritating traits and more besides, what the people of Hayle did to him on Carnival Day in the summer of 1978 was utterly shameful.

And when it became apparent that Dandy, who had absconded, was never coming back, it was Barbara Morethek who said, 'It's different now. Dandy was fun, he was a celebration. Like Christmas. I feel like all the glitter's gone out of Hayle. Do you know what I mean, Father?'

Father played a mournful bow across his larynx in agreement. And when Barbara, encouraged, repeated this mawkish observation to several acquaintances and it made the rounds of Hayle, heads shook at the thought of Carnival Day and there was a gloopy feeling of repentance in the air.

Until Barbara's words reached Tommy Wakfer up at the garage.

'The problem with Christmas,' said Tommy, 'is no fucker wants it every day of the year. And that's the problem with Dandy Allcock. He's all right about once every 365 days, but more than that and he gets on your tits. He's like Christmas in July: not right somehow.'

And Tommy's words did the rounds of Hayle and people tended to agree with his judgement, and the guilt at what happened to Dandy Allcock began to fade. Because words are powerful and Christmas in July seemed somehow to sum up Dandy Allcock perfectly, and made people shift their weight from one foot to the other and suck their teeth at the thought of him. Because he was like Christmas in July. He just didn't fit in.

***

The seeds of the Carnival Day incident were sown several months before, when Dandy had a bit of a tiffle with Ron Manor. Dandy was sitting at a table in the White Hart entertaining a couple of young men – tourists from Up Country he'd met at the bar – and telling them some marvellous stories about Hayle in the days of yore. And he was leaning into the table and shaking his G&T in his palm quite skilfully as he talked and – well! – those young men were enchanted to meet a local man who spoke so urbanely; and so he continued on and on, sipping or shaking his drink, introducing cheeky, almost daring, long pauses at richer moments in his monologue that demanded you swirl the facts about a bit before swallowing them.

'And so you see,' said Dandy, pointing at the young men, 'you never can know what to expect from a Hayle woman. Because for seventeen years Jessie Phillips dressed up as a man and left her idle and drunken husband in the house. There's a few of those in here I can tell you. Only joking. No I'm serious! No really, just joking: they're a good bunch in here, actually. Anyway, she left him in the house and went out to sea to put food on the family table.'

Dandy slapped his hand on the table, spilling G&T on the cuffs of his beige jumper. And, my goodness, there is something invigorating – it makes one alive! – to entertain and know that people are hanging on one's words. And Dandy's eyes glittered like a pair of sequins as the young men waited for more and, flushed with success and one too many G&Ts, he grinned, stood up – revealing a pipe-cleaner gait of long, angular limb, replete with riding shirtcuffs and just-too-short trousers – and clapped his hands very loudly indeed.

Clappety-clappety clap.

Loud, but rhythmic, you see. Nice. But, yes, quite loud, actually.

Because – oh, my giddy aunt – everyone stopped and looked at Dandy and Dandy looked back at all the staring heads and went:

'Ha ha ha ha ha ha!'

Were there a few dour Cornish cynics at the bar? Trouble in the front row? Best way to deal with that is to be really nice.

'Evening, gentlemen,' said Dandy, nodding at the assorted beards.

Nothing in reply, of course.

And Dandy, well, he had been full of it but he wished he'd kept quiet now. But there was no going back because they were all looking at him. Waiting.

'I say,' said Dandy. 'I thought it would be rather nice if I introduced these two young gentlemen to all assembled. They're on holiday, you see. Visiting us from Magdalen College. That's Oxford to you and me. But particularly to you, Ron.'

A few laughs. And laughter had the most peculiar effect on awkward-limbed Dandy: he loved it more than anything in the whole wide world. It made him grow taller, his skew-whiff limbs straightening out and his head stretching skywards like a flower feeling the warmth of the sun.

The young men shook hands with the beards at the bar and Dandy looked on proudly as his proteges made small talk with his peers.

'Your round is it, Dandy?' said Ron Manor, pinging the top of his pint with a chubby finger.

'My round?' said Dandy. He frowned at Ron and looked him up and down. 'My round?' And Ron frowned at Dandy and Dandy frowned at Ron. And then Dandy's eyebrows shot up and he went, 'Ha ha ha ha ha ha ha ha! My round is it? What are you having, Ron?'

And Ron, a chubby type with that fuzzy growth all over his neck, said, 'Pint.' Then he turned back to the bar, and didn't even acknowledge Dandy's friendly pat on the back.

And those young men from Magdalen – well! They had quite a way about them and were chatting to everyone and that's the nice thing about the truly well-educated, isn't it? Isn't it though? The way they can talk to anyone. It goes beyond social status with the well-educated, doesn't it?

And Dandy – no, don't get Dandy wrong – he could

lean on the bar and laugh at other people's anecdotes like the best of them. And he interjected with a 'They didn't?' and a 'Did they?' and several gasps and threw his head back and laughed and swirled his G&T quite loosely at his side. Yes, he could do all that. But Dandy did have a duty to say his piece, and it was beginning to weigh on him now. He had introduced the young men to the beards, you see. He was the compere, if you like. And right now he was in danger of losing control of his acts and his audience.

You could see the concern in Dandy's gait: he'd gone a bit stiff and his arm, which had been sloshing the G&T at hip level, began to bend and creep up his torso until finally his drink was clutched tight to his chest.

'Of course,' said Dandy, seizing on a momentary silence and wedging his body between the beards, 'Magdalen College was home to a veritable lion of the Victorian literary establishment. We're talking Wilde, of course.'

Dandy patted Ron Manor on the back. 'No, not Marty Wilde, Ron. Oscar Wilde.'

A few guffaws, augmented by a volley of 'ha ha ha ha ha has' from Dandy. And Dandy loosened his tie and stretched his neck towards the source of the warmth. It is nice, though, isn't it? It is nice to be appreciated.

Hey, but hang on one darned second there. Hold your horses! There's more mileage in this yet. Dandy's lips began to bubble and his tongue darted in and out of his mouth. 'He wrote, books, Ron,' he said as the laughter died away. 'Yes, books. You know, a bit more robust than a newspaper.'

And bellies swelled as heads rolled back and everyone was laughing and having a lovely time. And Dandy was rattling off his rapid-fire laugh, his face craning left and right on tortoise neck towards the source of the greatest warmth. Scrutinising. Because Dandy watched the beards with beady eyes, studying the laughter, hoarding it away.

It died. And the collective attention focused on the immobile figure sat at the bar. And though there was no face on view, intent observers – and Dandy was always an intent observer – may have noticed a twitching of the neck hair from Ron Manor. And Dandy braced himself for a little repartee with Ron, cocking his chest and throat, ready to pull the trigger on another volley of laughter. Dandy never understood what followed. Where was the wit in it? Where was the punnery, the inflection, the well-timed pause? There was none. And yet, briefly, it elicited far more laughter from the beards than anything Dandy had said tonight.

Ron Manor twisted the fuzzy neck and turned to face Dandy. And the face: so strikingly pink and gruesome it seemed independent of the body, like a severed pig's head in a butcher's.

'You?' he said, a greasy leer spreading over his face. 'You're a fucking cunt, you are.'

'Ha ha ha ha ha ha ha!' said Dandy.

And the beards threw back their heads and laughed. And Dandy continued to laugh, too, launching magazine after magazine, his body convulsing as he lost control. And soon the laughter died among the beards and they watched Dandy's performance with astonishment as he sprayed his hilarity around the room, his body recoiling with the force of urgent jocularity. And then their laughter started up again and they weren't laughing at Ron's put-down anymore, they were laughing at this… this strange, hysterical Dandy.

And Ron Manor looked on with a smudge of a grin on his face and everything seemed to be going his way until one of the young men said, 'Drink, Dandy?'

And Dandy caught the young man's eye and held to that gaze for dear life as he rattled out his laughter, swallowing deeper breaths as it began to slow down. Finally – what a relief! – it petered away altogether and Dandy finished off his performance with a bit of flaky coughing.

'Lovely,' said Dandy, and he mouthed G&T with a wink. And by the time he was handed his drink he'd regained control and become louder than even before, because he had allies now, friends. It was a remarkable turnaround.

In fact things went very well for Dandy as the evening progressed, though he couldn't help casting a glance at the cumulus on Ron Manor's neck – Ron was staring in at the bar again now – and look for some sign of his mood. Because it's nice for everyone to be included, isn't it? Isn't it though? I hate to think of someone not enjoying themselves, or being left out.

But Dandy could gauge nothing from Ron's neck and instead leaned in to him at the bar and said, 'I say, Ron. Can I get you another?'

But Ron didn't look at Dandy. His pig's head was sweating and he was boring holes into the peanuts and pork scratchings behind the bar. So Dandy left it at that. Though he felt some foreboding at Ron's silence.

And it's funny to think though, isn't it, that two peripheral characters in the life of Dandy Allcock, who showed a kindness to him virtually unknown in the wake of the habitual brutality he experienced in the pub, were partly responsible for the terrible revenge Ron Manor was to exact on him?

Dandy, who had done nothing more than get the upper hand over Ron in his own small way, who had survived the kind of put-down that should have crushed him and then gone on to claim the floor. In a way those two decent lads had helped destroy him. It is funny though, when you think about it, isn't it?

***

And yet there's something inexplicably sad about carnivals under grey Cornish skies. Something of the echo of fun, the echo of childhood, an experience half realised through the slit-eyed yawn of adulthood. A time when ungainly adults look down at children and feel only sorrow for the poor little bastards swizzled into believing life really was a carnival full of colour and mystery. And while the kids suck on ice-lollies and make orange moustaches, all the mums and dads see are the spent sticky wrappers hidden at the borders of the recreation ground in clumps of unmown grass. Everything about this loss of innocence was summed up in that yellow and pink outpost in the grey void: the ice-cream van. And leaning out of the van passing cornets to children, Harry Nuneater – signet-ringed and bald as a coot, his white coat stained with Neapolitan; a charming and mysterious presence for mums and dads when they were children: a potential paedophile threat now among those for whom cynicism had become the last refuge of their creativity.

And so on to the floats. All lined up for the judging before the procession. The madcap antics of the lads from the milk factory – dressed, inevitably, as St Trinian's schoolgirls – waning now, suffering skirt-lifting and bottle-squirting fatigue after an interminable grey-sky hour, several of them sitting, legs open, suspenders showing, and sucking on roll-ups, conserving madcappery for the procession later.

The taxi decorated with a few strings of tinsel, a miserable-looking Noreen Canker inside, infiltrating the carnival for a bit of free advertising. The fat-thighed majorettes goosepimpling in short skirts, the dusty old band with their shiny instruments, the rag-bag collection of oddly-dressed residents attired as unnameable and unplaceable characters or types, their identities lost somewhere in that gap between imagination and execution, looking like the mentally deficient left to dress themselves.

Terrible really. Crying children. Awful. Teetering – the whole thing teetering on the edge of some unknowable abyss, the playing field shimmering and becoming transparent and ghostly for moments at a time, as if it might fade and then disappear in one last ghastly echo and then there would be nothing.

And yet it held together. Somehow this event had a meaning, an overriding purpose that transcended the pockets of misty lassitude. And it was because of him over there, over yonder on the platform, that awkward, sparkling figure reading from a sheet of paper, fluffing lines over the Tannoy, full of cheer and authority and for this one day, this one day only, fully appreciated for his familiarity with the coattails of celebrity; because he had that... what is it... that... something... that thing that is so hard to describe but somehow gives an event some external, objective meaning, some association with write-ups in the paper.

That's it: there was a quality in Dandy's Allcock's narrative that had the self-assuredness of reflection, of finality before things are finished, of summation before things are summed up; there was a complacency in the tone that said: Yes, this is a carnival – it really is – just like people have all over Cornwall and England and this melancholy grey cast over the scene is nothing at all but a neutral backdrop to show off the glitter and the colours and when we look back at it all we will remember nothing but – ha ha ha ha ha ha ha! – a glorious day out for all.

It was Dandy's day.

'Is everyone having a lovely time? You are? Lovely! Won't be long now, folks, before the committee reaches its decision on the winning float. And hasn't it been a good year? Hasn't it, though? And before I forget, Mr Nuneater over at the ice-cream van – there he is: give us a wave Mr Nuneater. Lovely! – Mr Nuneater is offering any child in fancy dress two Milky Sticks for the price of one. On account of his freezer breaking down and everything melting. No, seriously folks. Just a joke. His fridges are marvellous. Hey. And moving on from fridges, I wonder which of our ice maidens will be crowned carnival queen this year? What's that? No, no, that's true: not ice maidens at all, but perfectly warm and friendly young maidens and I might add, Mrs Dorset, to put your mind at rest, that the word ice was employed only as a link – a segue, if you will – to move seamlessly from Mr Nuneater's freezers on to the young ladies. And, actually, Mrs Dorset, now I think of it, since I suggested Mr Nuneater's fridges were defective, I might well have been justified in segueing from Mr Nuneater's warm fridges to those warm-hearted maidens. No, Mr Nuneater. You misunderstood. I was just explaining to Mrs Dorset… What does it mean, Mrs Dorset? Segue means to proceed without any pause, something along those lines. Anyway, we are getting in a tangle here when the most important thing to ask is this: is everyone having a good time? Not a bad start, but a bit louder. Is everyone having a good time? That's better and if I'm not mistaken young Mark Drew has the finest set of lungs in the crowd. You beg to differ, Emily Penrose? Then let's hear it again: is everyone…'

And so on. A magnificent performance by Hayle

standards, so that even Dandy Allcock's detractors – at one time or another, most times in fact, pretty much everyone in Hayle – gave begrudging praise to this Dandy decked out in his special carnival coat with the purple sequins, those glittering jewels that sought out any trace of sun from the torpid sky and flashed and winked at the assembled crowd.

Dandy's day. A man who spent nearly every hour of his public life trying to understand the meaning of a cryptic code that was decipherable to everyone else in Hayle, who attempted to breeze and bluff his way through a labyrinth of signs and social meanings but inevitably faltered. No faltering today. Today Dandy spoke his own language. And people listened.

The judging went off marvellously, apart from a brief scene involving the St Trinian's crew when Meatball Simons – in yellow pigtails and black-dot freckles – slammed his waterbottle to the ground at the news that they had been beaten by Gossen Motors and their Little House On The Prairie. The water squirted from his bottle and soaked Superman – young Stevie Tompkin, that is – in the face, the subsequent tears from Stevie suggesting that soapy water now joined Kryptonite and magic in the list of the Man of Steel's vulnerabilities.

But it was a minor incident and Dandy was well pleased with the day as he stepped down from the podium and mingled with the crowd, nodding and smiling, receiving compliments, his hands behind his back and that untidy mess of limbs nice and straight now as he walked tall.

Lovely. A lovely day had by all and the smell of hot dogs and frying onions and – well, my word – when you thought about it, all false modesty aside, he really had played a significant role in setting the tone for the day, geeing people up a bit, introducing a few jokes, pausing for effect as he announced the winners.

Oh look over there, isn't that Ron Manor and a few of the beards from the White Hart? Shall I? No, better not, they look quite busy and serious. Best leave the lads to their own... Me? I didn't know if you were pointing at me or someone behind me? Thanks very much, Ron, it did all go off rather well, didn't it? Splendid? You really are too kind. Drink? Well, I don't know really, Ron, it is rather early for me but... yes, I do like a G&T, you've noticed have you. Ha ha ha ha ha ha ha! Oh go on then, in for the proverbial penny as they say. They don't? They say: In for a penny? Ah, yes I do see your point. But I do have a sneaking suspicion you're making fun of me. No, not at all. Marvellous in fact. I love a bit of fun. A bit of fun is lovely, isn't it though? Really very nice indeed!

And so off trudged Dandy to his doom, leading the beards with his long strides towards the Copperhouse. Although indirectly, because Ron insisted that he was buggered if he was going to the Copperhouse without buying Tracy Rosewarne, the Carnival Queen herself, a pint of bitter.

No, no, said Tracy. Oh, all right then. And Dandy insisted on lifting her train for her all the way, because it was rather muddy. Some of the beards, in their good humour, encouraged Dandy to lift it a bit higher so they could get a look at those suspenders. And he did and they were treated to the sheen of stocking and a white, flaccid thigh that threatened to spill like an overflowing head on a beer.

And do you know? Dandy was feeling a bit squiffy after his second G&T. No, honestly, he was. A bit tight, as Mother used to say. But they were all having a marvellous time sitting around the table sharing a few stories.

'And so Mother took the buns out of the oven,' said Dandy. 'And she said to Father, "What on earth?" Like that, very screechy Mother was when she was on her high horse about something. And she said, "Bryan, what on earth is this black stuff all over my buns?" And Father, he looked at Mother's buns and said, "Just a cursory glance, Mother" – he was a one, Father was – "Just a cursory glance suggests coffee icing to me." Well, now Mother – dear old Mother – she stared at him something awful, poked her finger at the black stuff on the buns and said, "Father, where are your Wellington boots?" And Father said, "Mother, what on earth has that to do with your buns?" And Mother said, "Father, it has everything to do with my buns". And swiftly she pulled the oven open to reveal a pair of Wellingtons on the top grill dripping down to the tray below. Ha ha ha ha ha ha ha! Marvellous though, isn't it? Father loved a drink. Must have come in a bit tight the night before, I should imagine. Not a word of apology to Mother, either. For years afterwards he would say, "Mother, you are a very good cook, that's indisputable. But I never did take to your rubber buns."'

And Dandy slapped his G&T on the table and soaked his sequined cuffs and the beards roared with laughter, their heads thrown back; even Ron Manor was roaring away, his head red and sweating. A close-knit group full of jittering beards and perspiring pink skin it was. Really nice. Everyone really enjoying themselves. Marvellous.

But Dandy had to think about moving on because there was the little matter of seeing the floats out in the correct order, and spacing the majorettes and the band out a bit to make sure they didn't bunch up in a pile of brass and thighs like last year.

'Fuck that,' said Ron, grinning at Dandy. 'If I can't

buy the man who makes Hayle carnival happen another large gin and tonic, I don't know what the world is coming too.' Ron turned to Tracy. 'Another pint for you too, my lover?'

Tracy, who was sweating – she looked a bit put upon by the alcohol – nodded and so there they were, at it again: the tight-knit group getting tighter all the time, faces closer and pinker, pores in skin gaping, the flashing lights of the jukebox throbbing in reds and greens and purples, the ejaculations of laughter, the heads dropping back and the fountains of blue smoke squirting up into the air.

'Ha ha ha ha ha ha ha!' went Dandy. 'I really must visit the little boy's room.'

And the beards roared with laughter at that. It was all in the delivery, you see. And Ron Manor explained how he had given up smoking four years ago to the day and Dandy said it was 12 years for him and well that set them off again, beards splitting in two and pink mouths stretched wide in mirth and Tracy just fell off her stool, no she's back up again now, and Ron is bringing her another pint and a gin and tonic for Dandy and well you can try and you can try but sometimes things just prick I mean click and Dandy is laughing and laughing and laughing his face bright red and his teeth all yellow in the mirror and for the life of him he can't remember what he's laughing at and that makes him cry but he knows he's crying in happiness and then he's standing in the corridor by the toilet talking to Ron and Ron has his arm around him and Dandy feels light as a feather and Ron is saying I've always liked you to be honest Dandy you're a decent sort of bloke and I'm glad we've had the chance to chat like this and we shall have one more just the one more mind you no don't be silly you're fine my handsome just a bit tiddly that's all and don't worry about that they'll clear that up what do you think they're paid for for Christ's sake?

**

Dandy dreamt of gulls. But the gulls had human faces. Rows and rows of human faces passing him by in a procession, smiling, burbling, squawking. It was a long time before Dandy realised he wasn't dreaming anymore. It was even longer before he realised the faces weren't part of a procession. He was.

People. Bill Cornish, Richard Pearce, Grace Pellow, Barry Trembath, Maggie Bern and hundreds more, all laughing and pointing at Dandy. Faces Dandy knew and faces he didn't know. And along with the laughter came the sound of the band parping and clashing just up ahead – parp, clash, parp, clash, parp parp, clash.

Dandy's head was in a terrible fog, but there was nothing to do but rise to the occasion, so he lifted his arm and began to wave. And, do you know, the laughter got louder as Dandy's arm swayed back and forth; and he felt his body fill with a vigorous, joyous energy, so he waved all the harder, his limp arm movements giving way to a frenetic wave that was all in the wrist. He craned his head towards the pavement and to the source of the laughter and a smile spread across his face.

Because, for a moment, Dandy felt the hum of his self bursting through the confines of his body, filling out his flesh like it never had before. The laughter was feeding him and he felt not merely among the people of Hayle – a part of Hayle – but greater than the people of Hayle; greater in a way he had never dared imagine before. His body became erect and his chin jutted forth, and his curls all danced together in one motion as he jolted along, like a troop of pouffed-up soldiers for a great parade. For one moment Danny felt this. For one sublime moment.

Then something changed. A low rumble reached him, a sound that hurbled and burbled way beneath the laughter and the shrieks. It had been there all the time, but Dandy only recognised it now as it gained momentum and grew louder; and weren't some of the faces now turning away from Dandy and sharing their laughter with each other?

The hurble burble and the conspiratorial faces made Dandy self-conscious of his waving hand, which brought his attention to the layers of chiffon – itchy white chiffon – that covered his arms. Dandy followed the chiffon up to his shoulder. Then he looked down his chest at the frills and the trims and the pouffed-up layers. He reached a hand instinctively to his head. Yes, it was there, too: itchy, scratchy: a headdress. And that hurble burble, rising and rising in Dandy's ears, had all the sound of scandal. Dandy looked around him. He was sitting in a bowl, layered with quilts and feathers. And behind him, above him, leaning over him, another bowl. No, not a bowl: a shell. A clam shell. Dandy was a chiffon-clad pearl in a clam shell.

He looked at his arm. It was waving harder than ever. He looked out at the sea of faces.

'Ha ha ha ha ha ha!' went Dandy. Because Dandy loved nothing more than a bit of laughter.

'Ho ho ho ho ho ho! went the crowd, and, 'burble, hurble burble.'

Dandy watched the faces pass by as the procession reached the harbour. People burbled and glanced and spoke to one another with their eyes. And the children pointed at him as they laughed. And Dandy was cornered in a way that few people are ever cornered, and briefly knew himself with a clarity few people suffer. There were no illusions now. People mocked; and Dandy laughed.

Dandy felt a raw sting on his cheek. He clutched his face and looked up. The crowd roared. And there was Tommy Wakfer high above, leaning out of his workshop window smiling down at Dandy. And now Tommy had his pipe to his lips – the copper peashooter that was the scourge of every misfit in Hayle – and was aiming at Dandy again. His cheeks puffed. Nothing. He had missed. But the burbling crowd swelled; then it roared. And Dandy felt a sharp blow to the back of his head that sent him flying into layers of clam shell chiffon. He swung around. There, swaying above him, dressed in Dandy's trousers and purple-sequined jacket stood deposed carnival queen Tracy Rosewarne, rubbing her sleepy face with her hand and swearing at Dandy silently amid the roar of the crowd. A monster woken by Tommy's stray putty bullet.

'Ha ha ha ha ha ha ha! went Dandy.

'You cheeky bastard,' mouthed Tracy, launching herself at the usurper and ripping his headdress off.

And Dandy and Tracy wrestled in the clam shell as the float approached the viaduct and Foundry Square. Quite enthusiastically they wrestled, too, because soon the upper half of the shell came crashing down on them and as good as closed the clam altogether, but for the odd flailing limb poking through.

And people swore afterwards – though how they could have heard above the laughter, it's hard to say – that you could still hear Dandy laughing in that shell. A muffled Dandy, but the distinctive sound of Dandy all the same.

'Ha ha ha ha ha ha ha!'

courtesy calls and quality biscuits

'I DON'T CARE what you say, Mrs Pellow. I've heard them talking up the station about this new one or that new one, but I'm having none of it. As far as I'm concerned, you can't beat a HobNob. Honestly, you can say what you like, Mrs Pellow.'

But Mrs Pellow wasn't saying anything. And though PC Thomas' passionate rhetoric seemed to put her firmly in the anti-HobNob camp, her rhythmic munching suggested otherwise.

And the pair of them sat opposite each other at the table, masticating in the clock-tick quiet of mid-morning Boskennal Drive.

'Lovely,' said PC Thomas.

'It is a nice biscuit,' said Mrs Pellow. 'There's no denying that.'

PC Thomas took a sip of his tea to clear his palette. He shifted on his buttocks and looked around the room. There was silence for a moment, and apparently a lack of will on the policeman's part to fill it.

'Oh,' said Mrs Pellow. 'Would you like another one?'

PC Thomas looked surprised. 'No thank you, my lover.' He patted a hard belly. 'I've got my diet to think of, see.'

'I wouldn't have thought a biscuit would hurt.'

PC Thomas seemed to weigh this up for a minute. 'No,' he said. 'I suppose it wouldn't.' And with that he took another HobNob and munched away.

'And it is a lovely bit of biscuit,' he said.

Mrs Pellow pecked away at hers. 'Is it sweet or salty would you say, PC Thomas?'

Alas, it was too late. Because with a little squeak of a swallow PC Thomas's biscuit was on the way to his stomach to join the five others that wouldn't hurt.

'Sweet or salty?' he said, squinting into the middle distance, perhaps to disassociate himself from a chubby hand that was plucking another biscuit from the packet. 'Sweet or salty, sweet or salty?' He munched away on the fresh biscuit and then swallowed. 'I would say, Mrs Pellow, there was something of sweet and saltiness in it, wouldn't you?'

Mrs Pellow nibbled, her eyes darting about the walls as she considered. 'I think you're right,' she said. 'And do you know what's funny, PC Thomas? I might have thought about that all day and wondered which it was. But I should never in my life have realised it was both.'

'All part of the service. It's my job to get to the bottom of things. To evaluate quickly.'

PC Thomas pointed a fresh biscuit at the air. He looked thoughtful. 'Though that's not to say I'm comparing tasting a biscuit to solving crime. That would be ridiculous.'

And ridiculous PC Thomas certainly was not. He had served 23 years as a policeman in Hayle. And in all that time there had been very little trouble to speak of. You had your drunks, of course, and your odd flasher. You had that Clint Morris always looking for a fight and your occasional burglary or stolen car. You had they sods coming out of The Penmare on a Saturday night and jumping in the open-air swimming pool. Crowds of them some nights. But in all fairness it's never easy taking details in the dark and how was PC Thomas to know that Denzil Hendrix and Demelza Bowie were made up names? All in all, you could say PC Thomas had seen all that crime had to offer a small Cornish town. But he had never before heard of a break-in where the perpetrator merely ate from a selection – a rather discerning selection, in PC Thomas' opinion – of quality biscuits.

'Anyway, Mrs Pellow, I didn't come here to eat biscuits.'

'Just one more.'

'Go on then, last one. But I'm here to tell you we're on to the chap who did this.'

'Oh lovely. What have you found?'

'Found?'

'I mean what clues have you discovered, PC Thomas?'

'Clues!' PC Thomas dipped his mouth into his jowls and laughed. 'My dear life, Mrs Pellow, this isn't Sherlock Holmes. I haven't got a magnifying glass.'

'I find them very handy for reading the paper.'

'I'm sure you do. But don't you worry about clues and the such like. Leave it to the experts. I've got three men on this case, three good men. In fact, I think you know young Steven Green.'

'Audrey's Steven? She was worried when they put him back a year at school.'

'Rest assured, my dear. He's come on lovely.'

'Dick Elliot said, "Poor old Audrey. That boy will come to nothing."'

'He's a policeman now, Mrs Pellow.'

'You see, Dick was right about Sheila Morris' boy, too. Dick said, "I'll tell you now, Sheila, and you mark my words. That Clint is going to be trouble. I can see it in his eyes. He's a fighter."'

'But back to the biscuits, Mrs Pellow. We've got an important lead.'

'A lead? Is that like a clue?'

'It is something like a clue, only it's more useful. It

goes somewhere.' PC Thomas held up his palms. 'And don't ask me what it is, Mrs Pellow, because we can't divulge at this juncture. Just rest assured, we'll get the burglar.'

'He's a burglar then?' said Mrs Pellow.

'Of course he's a burglar. He broke into your house.'

'But he didn't steal anything. He just ate a few biscuits.'

'But don't you feel violated? A stranger in your home?'

Mrs Pellow looked surprised. 'I suppose I do.' She nibbled at a biscuit.

'You can't blame him, though. I do keep a lovely selection of biscuits.'

'They are lovely biscuits,' said PC Thomas. Because there was no denying that.

'Have you tried a chocolate finger?' said Mrs Pellow.

'I don't believe I have.'

'Oh, my dear life. My favourite! A nice dry finger of a biscuit. Do you know what I mean by dry? Very crunchy. And dipped in milk chocolate. I do dearly love a bit of milk chocolate.' Mrs Pellow got up. 'Promise me you'll stay right there, PC Thomas. I'll be back in a moment.'

But she needn't have worried: PC Thomas was going nowhere. Hayle constabulary had the happy luxury of being able to approach their work at a leisurely pace. Where forces in rougher parts of the land – Camborne for instance – were swamped with petty crimes and paperwork, the Hayle boys had time for analysis, to chew over a case, to let the facts digest a little.

Mrs Pellow was back with a tray of chocolate fingers. 'Now, you try one of these and tell me what you think.'

PC Thomas broke into peals of laughter. He shook his head and pushed her hand away. 'No, Mrs Pellow. This really is outrageous.' And Mrs Pellow, perhaps feeling the force of his objection, did start to move the tray away. 'Absolutely outrageous,' chortled PC Thomas, shaking his head and lifting his arse off the seat to grab a handful of fingers from the receding tray. 'My goodness me,' he said, forcing a finger into his mouth and chewing away.

'Well?' said Mrs Pellow.

PC Thomas munched in silence. Mrs Pellow waited.

'As you say,' he said, still munching, 'rather brittle and dry. But a pleasant texture when complemented with the milk chocolate, which does tend to lubricate matters.

'Furthermore,' he said, wagging a chocolate finger at Mrs Pellow, 'I would say a fairly high proportion of cocoa solids, which makes for better-quality chocolate.'

Quite a performance, it was. Mrs Pellow looked on with admiration. 'I knew you'd like it,' she said. 'Talented you are. Summed it up lovely. And do you know what I think, PC Thomas? The chap who burgled my house hasn't got a chance against a man who can get to the bottom of a biscuit like you can.'

PC Thomas looked askance at Mrs Pellow. But there was no craft in the woman. Not that PC Thomas could detect.

'But there is one thing that's been on my mind,' said Mrs Pellow. 'It was on TV the other week. Do you watch *Tales Of The Unexpected*, PC Thomas?'

'I have seen it now and again.'

'A few weeks back, a woman murdered her husband. Now, the police came around to have a chat and console her, because they didn't know she did it, of course. She insisted they have something to eat, and she gave them a lovely bit of lamb. Nice great joint it was. There they are eating away. And the people who write these programmes are clever. Some clever they are. Because do you know what the police had done?'

PC Thomas had no idea.

'They'd eaten the evidence. Because she killed her husband by hitting him over the head with that very leg of lamb. When it was still frozen, of course.'

PC Thomas took a moment to digest the facts. But no, they wouldn't settle.

'I wouldn't have thought,' he said with an anxious swallow, 'it would be possible to clobber someone with a packet of biscuits.'

Mrs Pellow laughed. 'A card you are. And dry!' But she looked serious again. 'No, what I mean is, I hope we're not eating the evidence.'

PC Thomas sat up and straightened his spine. His hand reached instinctively for another chocolate finger and pushed it at his pursed lips while he considered matters. He shook his head. 'No, Mrs Pellow, I shouldn't worry. It's good of you to take an interest in procedure, but there's nothing to worry about. You enjoy your biscuits.' And with that he popped the pensive finger into his mouth, brushed the considerable mound of crumbs from his lap and got up. 'Thank you very much for the tea and biscuits. I shouldn't have really, what with my diet. But if we have any more news on your case, I shall pop by.'

'I'm sure you will,' said Mrs Pellow. 'And I thought next time we might try a Boaster.'

And with that they exchanged their final pleasantries and PC Thomas was back on the streets of Hayle, walking down Foundry Hill with a leisurely stroll, lingering at the Millpond to throw some sharp looks at teenagers, and bringing a fist to his mouth outside the White Hart as evidence began to repeat on him.

love and ice-cream

AT THE BLEAKEST hour of Sunday, he comes. At that very moment when lunch is over and a little silence marks the start of a long and pointless afternoon. Never mind that lunch is enjoyed at different times across Hayle, or that his lugubrious rounds cover nine estates over a period of two hours, still, by some diabolical magic, his arrival is perfectly timed in every household to follow the dropping of final fork on plate.

Greensleeves, through speakers so distorted it crackles, bending through the air as the van passes by. Once – at least three owners ago in the van's long history – the tune charmed children and they ran into the street with ice-cream glee. Now it is so worn it has a bitter edge, like regretful laughter when remembering joys long gone. It is the sound of childhood and childhood lost altogether.

And should a child, its ear not yet attuned to tragedy, jump up from the table and beg its mother for ice-cream, it is placated by one of those small deceits that harbour children from the harsh realities of adulthood.

'No, my lover. That tune means he's run out of ice-cream.'

Yet in a garden – oh no! – an unattended child is lured if not by the crackling melody then by the pinks and blues of the little van and approaches Henry Caldwell, philosopher and ice-cream vendor of the apocalypse.

'And what, young man, can I do for you today?' says Henry, grinning with a thin, wide smile.

The young man orders a 99 and Henry selects a

cone, frowning as he holds it up to the light, daring it to present him with a defect. Satisfied, he reaches down with his scoop into the bowels of his freezer, his head on its side resting upon the edge. Out comes the cone sporting a blob of vanilla ice-cream so small it threatens to drop into the void and disappear, which it does by the time Henry spears it with a chocolate flake.

He reaches out of the van to hand the ice-cream to the child. The child reaches to take it. Henry pulls his hand away.

'A question, my young friend.' Henry holds up the ice-cream. 'Here we have a 99. But what, do you think, would it take to make it 100?'

Silence. What kind of question is this for a child? A 99 is a 99, it is a thing completed, an object of joy, like the sky or a bird. Suddenly there is the possibility of a 97, a 98 or that diabolical 100, and one can hear the clanking of pistons and the hiss of steam from somewhere beneath the world of finished objects.

The fridge hums. The child looks at it nervously. Perhaps in its depths lurks the dreadful thing that will make his 99 a 100? Or take something away and make it a 96.

An intellectual equal of Henry, with a touch of the wag thrown in, might well remark that his 99 barely warrants a 39 when you consider the parsimonious portion. And yet the child quivers before the great philosopher and looks as if he might burst into tears.

'Just a bit of fun,' says Henry, handing him the ice-cream. He looks at the child with eyes of deadly intent. 'Mind how you go.'

And the child, who had been going quite marvellously all morning, kicking his football and cavorting about the garden with an abandon that suggested more Saturday afternoon than empty Sunday, does begin to mind rather too much as he goes, his little head bending to footsteps that lack all the intelligence and poetry of unconscious movement now and take on the dull stupidity of minding and knowing.

Henry starts up the van and moves on, hunting for customers.

***

Something in Henry, in every word or action, was bent on revealing the winter of frigid disappointments that is adulthood. He considered it a duty, almost, an act of kindness; and yet there was a little cruelty in it, and a little too much enthusiasm, too.

'I will tell you this, Steven,' he said one day. 'You are happy with her now, but at the end of the summer she will leave for university. Distance, along with a surfeit of attractive young men, will take its toll on your relationship and it will end. That is the natural order of things and I tell you as a friend and as a man who knows.'

And Steven, so tall and pink and grinning in his rugby shirt, seemed to age as Henry spoke, lines creeping over his face as he squinted and frowned.

Young people paid the highest price for Henry's ice-cream. They paid with their innocence.

Henry must be stopped. He must be rehabilitated. And there is just one thing that will repair a bitter man broken on the jagged rocks of the world. And that, of course, is love.

***

Did fate bring love to Henry as an act of kindness to the people of Hayle? Who knows? Who cares? Why step into the bowels of the world and examine the honking, clanking machinery with its bursts of hot steam and pistons and hammers when there is so much that is wonderful up above? Why indeed, Henry?

She came to him on a grey and blowy March day, while Henry sat in the car park at Godrevy looking out over Godrevy Lighthouse.

Business, of course, was bad. Although this gave Henry the satisfaction of knowing the world just as it is, with all its toil and disappointments, it also gave him considerable anxiety with regard to his mortgage.

'Excuse me?'

Henry looked towards the counter. A ruddy, attractive woman of 35 or so stood below him, her cheeks puffing, the sweat running off her temples.

'How can I help you?' said Henry, his thin smile plumping up a little at the sight of her.

'You can't help me, my lover,' she said. 'I'm here to help you.'

Henry looked behind him. He turned back to face her. 'Me?' He pointed at his chest. 'I'm afraid I am beyond all redemption.'

'Then you haven't tasted my blueberry burst ice-cream,' she said. She opened the plastic bucket at her feet and handed Henry a small tub. Henry opened the tub and sniffed.

'You can eat it, too,' she said, grinning.

'No doubt,' said Henry. 'But I am not sure I can cope with the happy violence of a blueberry burst.'

He dipped the spoon into the ice-cream and tasted.

'Interesting,' he said. 'A simple cream, sugar, fruit puree recipe but with 40 if not 45 per cent sugar. Am I right?'

'I don't know,' she said. 'I just throw the buggers together, dip my finger in and taste it.'

'I would say 45 per cent sugar.' Henry pointed a finger at her. 'Now, the blueberry has a natural mustiness, a dimness – a dusk about it you might say – that is missing here, on account of the excess sugar. In fact, when I was experimenting, I toyed with naming one of my own ice-creams blueberry gloom.'

'You can call it what you like,' she said. 'But do you like the flavour and will you buy six litres off me?'

Henry frowned. 'Do I like the flavour?' he asked himself. He tasted again and ran his tongue about his mouth. 'No,' he said emphatically. 'No I don't believe I do. It is too optimistic.'

'Optimistic?' She grinned at him. 'You tuss.'

'Besides,' said Henry. 'I make my own ice-cream and I only sell vanilla.'

She shook her head. 'Optimistic,' she said again. And with that she picked up her bucket and heaved off across the field, laughing as she went.

Henry watched her trudge away in her wellies. She was still shaking with laughter.

'What an extraordinary woman,' he said, smiling. He checked himself and frowned. 'What an extraordinarily daft woman.'

***

Two months later Henry found himself two months closer to exhausting his savings and two months nearer to losing his little home. And the only thing that stood between him and disaster was the most beautiful vanilla ice-cream in the world. No one made ice-cream like Henry. Not anymore. He made it just as it should be made – traditionally. First he created a custard from cream, milk, sugar, eggs and vanilla pods, the simplest, purest recipe based on 18th Century tastes. Then he filled the outer compartment of his maple-finished, hand-cranked ice-cream maker with rock ice and salt, to get a below freezing temperature, and poured his custard into the central compartment. Now the real work began. Henry turned and turned the crank, folding in the custard which grew colder and colder and thickened into ice-cream. He sweated. He stopped frequently to mop his brow, lest his sweat contaminate the mixture. He grunted. His biceps and forearms grew red and throbbed.

At first, twelve months ago, he hadn't noticed the stress on his body. He was fond of waxing lyrical on the noble tradition of ice-cream as he worked the crank, calling out the names of ancients who were lovers of the cold confection, from the Emperor Nero to King Tang of China. Bursts of charm from his former life – a charm that had so delighted his students – came out at such times. These days, his arms were just tired and he saw perfection for the cold tyrant it was. Henry had learned much in recent months. He had learned that he did not like his ice-cream any more. He did not even sample it – he knew what it would taste like. He knew it to be the perfect combination of cream, sugar, eggs and vanilla churned just so. He knew everything there was to know about it and paradoxically it had become both the perfect ice-cream and also a well-measured collection of commonplace ingredients. It was everything, but it was also nothing. Of course the most perfect ice-cream in the world is expensive to make. Henry's portions were so small they peeked tentatively over the tops of cones. In a curious way he was satisfied by this. He knew that the more beautiful something becomes, the more elusive it becomes, and the less satisfied it is to remain in this unsatisfactory corporeal world.

***

Brutish ice-cream lickers, on the other hand, knew nothing of beauty and perfection. They wanted big portions at a cheap price. And she was giving it to them.

Henry watched from his van as she lurched about the car park at Godrevy with her tub by her side. At this time of year many families sat in their cars and watched the sea. She walked among them, grinning, leaning into windows, joking and serving up top heavy ice-creams that dripped and melted and ran through fingers so quickly it was all over the customer's hands before they had time to lick. And Henry had nothing to do but watch. She was a big woman, but she was not fat. He hair shone blue black in the spring sunshine. Her eyes were green. On sunny mornings she began to glisten and strokes of black hair stuck to her forehead.

Henry watched and watched. And he thought to himself that there is nothing so sad as something that is almost beautiful, something that both evokes beauty and is a pantomime of beauty.

Henry was a thinker, a philosopher. And from his lonely outpost at Godrevy car park, with cows grazing on the hills behind, and the blue sea frothing white on the shiny rocks below, he looked across to stately Godrevy Lighthouse and thought of beasts and angels and mankind's curious lot between; and about how a woman could make him think of everything that is happy and sad about the world.

'Here we have a 99,' said Henry to a boy, the first customer of the day. 'What do you think would make 100?'

The young man, unperturbed by the question, frowned at the meagre portion handed to him. 'Another scoop of ice-cream?' he said.

'Another scoop of ice-cream,' repeated Henry.

'Marvellous,' he said, closing the hatch and leaving

the child staring at the meagre portion while he carefully counted the silver and bronze coins that made up the first takings of the day.

He looked through the glass and watched her. He felt a strange attraction for her, coupled with a revulsion that came over him like hot, sweet breath. His skin prickled under his white coat. He felt clammy. It was a warm day.

***

One grey, cloudy day she was working near the van. Henry called her over. He nodded towards Godrevy Lighthouse.

'I should rather like to spend a month over there,' he said. 'Just to see what it is like.'

'In your van?' she said.

'How would I ever get it over there?' said Henry. 'No, I would live in the lighthouse, looking back towards the land. I believe I'd be quite happy.'

'I couldn't stand it,' she said. 'I had a friend who worked from home. It was lonely and it turned her head.'

'I notice your ice-creams melt rather quickly,' said Henry.

'I can't get them cold enough,' she said.

'It has nothing to do with the temperature. It's the recipe.'

'I never knew that.'

'There's a lot you don't know about making ice-cream.'

'And a lot you don't know about selling it.'

'It has occurred to me that if we joined forces we should do rather well.'

'Work together?'

'It makes sense,' said Henry. 'I know how to make ice-cream and you have a natural charm with the customers. Working the van together, all around Hayle, we could sell vanilla ice-cream by the tubful.'

'And blueberry, honeycomb and Smarties flavours.'

Henry grinned.

'Just vanilla.'

'What's the sense in that? More flavours, more choice, more sales.'

'A confection loaded with Smarties or honeycomb is not an ice-cream at all,' said Henry. 'It is a cluster of cheap sweets glued together.'

'People like it.'

'People need educating.'

She threw back her head and laughed. 'Educating? They don't need educating, you tuss – they need filling up.'

***

They compromised. They sold Henry's vanilla and her own creations, toned down somewhat to suit Henry's tastes.

Henry made a big fuss of not trying her flavours. 'It is enough that I agree to participate in such atrocities. Tasting them is out of the question.'

Her name was Sarah. She dipped her finger in the tubs and licked.

She said it was hard to know when he was being serious. He never seemed sincere, real.

'I just don't believe you,' she said.

'There is such a thing as robbing a story of its reality by making it too true,' he said. He pointed at her. 'Who said that?'

'Probably Oscar Wilde.'

Henry grinned. 'How do you know?'

'Maybe I'm not as stupid as you think.'

'Perhaps not.'

'You cheeky bastard,' she said.

They got on well. Business picked up. They worked together in the van. Sometimes Sarah heaved a bucket of ice-cream among the parked cars. Henry watched her. It was complicated. He enjoyed her company, but he felt guilty at the way hours passed easily. He longed for a noble loneliness, a dignified loneliness that would thrust him up close to the true matter of the world. He felt he was giving something up. It occurred to him that people give up with a simple smile and a shrug those very things that make them special. She had given them up. And yet he saw something in her eyes, those quick green eyes that would look towards Godrevy Lighthouse – just as Henry did, for noble thoughts are drawn towards noble, lonely objects – as if drinking in the quiet revelation that though the day-to-day world we live in is chatter and smiles and crosswords and television there is a terrible, beautiful truth beyond that is the heart of the matter. A noble truth. And we must not be cowards. We must live in it.

And then she would cast off the thought, her big teeth growing in her big mouth as she smiled at customers, her eyes flickering from one thing to another as before. Losing herself in everyday people and objects.

***

In the evenings, Sarah helped him make the ice-cream. And what a thing it was to see him in the throws of physical labour. He was grim and full of the burden of a great responsibility one moment, and exhilarated the next. One might imagine that Henry – his T-shirt damp with sweat, his biceps and forehead red and stinging – was turning the very world with that little handle.

'We should get electric machines,' said Sarah.

Henry stopped turning and looked up.

'And have light, frothy ice-cream with no texture or integrity?'

'Integrity?' she said. And she turned away and her shoulders began to shake with laughter.

Henry began turning again, faster and faster.

He stopped again.

'All right, we'll try it,' he said. 'But I guarantee it won't work.'

It worked. And Henry was amazed at what she could throw away with the merest shrug and smile.

***

One grey summer's day, they parked in Foundry Square. The viaduct loomed over the little row of shops. Rain crackled on the roof of the van. All colour was washed from the world. They leaned on the fridge and looked out. Henry felt restless. He was not content. The day before had been sunny, beautiful. They had talked and talked and gazed at Godrevy Lighthouse. He was growing more and more fond of her. And yet now – this silence and this rain. A world that was whole had broken into fragments. He felt the need to fix it. So he did what he knew would entertain her, make her laugh: he rebuilt the world, and made something better of it than the washed-out grey of Hayle on a rainy afternoon.

And Old Bastards Dick Elliot and Arthur Tredinnick over in the doorway of the bakery were not endlessly raking up past indignities as their fellow townsfolk happened by – that great roll call of infidelities, breakdowns, minor drugs offences and drink-driving convictions – but were two philosophers, and sceptics of a different kind.

'And yet, Dick,' said Arthur, 'take away light and do the objects of this world exist? For are we not seeing a concept – an interplay between light and matter – and not a true object at all.'

'And we might go further,' said Dick. 'Let us remove all senses – sight, touch, taste, smell, hearing. What of those objects now?'

And Henry rubbed the steamed up window as he spoke, making a porthole so she could properly see the two misanthropes doubting the world in the most improbable and yet somehow characteristic way. It was as if he had taken their very essences and recast them as intellectuals.

Henry made more portholes. They saw PC George Thomas, local hardman Clint Morris, Tommy Wakfer and others, and together acted out little routines and stories that brought the town to life in a fresh new way. And the grey world crackled as rain hit the roof and Sarah laughed and said it was like watching footage recorded a long time ago.

Henry created another porthole and they looked across the square to Charles Tresize and Barbara Morethek in their fruit shack. And he was silent as he watched those strange, silent lovers looking over the square as the rain fell in long ropes from the shack's awning.

His mouth felt dry from all the talking. His head hummed. And as he wiped his palm over the windows and cleared the glass, he remembered other times when the objects of Foundry Square were scattered in wide empty space. Times when he was happy that way: a man in a lonely wilderness, free.

The afternoon wore on. No customers came.

'The problem,' said Sarah, 'is that the portions are too small. And the portions are too small because you insist on the best eggs and farm-fresh cream. Give them something cheaper and we'll sell more.'

Henry nodded his head. He was exhausted. After a while he said, 'I think we'll finish early today.'

The next day he told her their ice-cream aesthetics were incompatible.

Sarah asked him if he really had just said 'ice-cream aesthetics'. She asked him if he was serious. He said yes. She laughed and walked away.

***

Life went on. Henry was lonely and free. But he wasn't happy.

A few months later he saw her at Godrevy, hobbling about between the cars with her ice box. He drove the van towards her and came to a stop in her path.

'How's business?' he said, leaning out of the hatch.

'Pretty good,' she said.

'And your ice-creams are maintaining their integrity.'

'They are. But they will never compete with you in that department.'

'You can't deny,' said Henry, 'that my recipe has been extremely helpful to you.'

'Would you like a small percentage?'

'Don't be ridiculous.'

'Let's say 10 per cent.'

'I don't want a percentage.'

'Suit yourself.'

It was a beautiful October and yet all of autumn, sweet and syrupy autumn, was about her. She was in all things. Henry parked on housing estates and watched the golden goings-on of children chasing about on bikes and kicking balls and there was poetry, something magnificent and profound, in their cries and laughter in this world of gold and blue.

It was all an illusion, of course: the manifestation of a great yearning. Henry remembered that as the days grew unspeakably beautiful.

***

He clung to what he knew. To the old routines.

'A question, young man,' he said one day. 'Here we have a 99, composed of cone, ice-cream and flake.'

Henry began to wag a finger at the boy. 'And yet how shall we apportion the various parts with value, how shall we make our 99?' Henry grinned. 'Shall we afford the cone 19 per cent, the flake 30 and the ice-cream 50?'

He leaned out of the window and handed the cone to the child. And though the boy did frown and squint at Henry's questions, the brutish tongue was already licking away without the slightest doubt that a 99 was not an object assembled and counted into existence by the hand of man, but a thing completed from the moment the thought of it entered his little mind, ready to be licked to oblivion. And furthermore, even as the flake and then the ice-cream disappeared and that very last piece of cone was ready to be popped into his mouth, he did not squint with any scepticism. He believed fully in the myth of manifested objects. It was a 99 from start to finish. Such was the faith of children. And men and women, who behaved like children.

When the child had gone, Henry made himself an ice-cream and held it in front of his eyes. He squinted and gave it such a curious, scrutinising look any potential customer at the hatch – there were none, of course – might well have had serious doubts about purchasing ice-cream from a vendor who gave his wares such forensic examination. He tasted it. It disappointed him. He knew it down to the merest gram of sugar. He thought of Sarah. Of all the things he didn't know about her.

And still the sun rose and fell on golden October and though Henry knew it was a passing season, and the glee of children was a passing glee in this Indian summer, he felt the poetry of small things move through his chest like heartburn. It might be a seagull up above, drifting in the sky; an old car rocking and bucking on a dirt track to the beach, its powdery blue exhaust fumes hanging in the still autumnal air; a V of golden sunlight on tarmac in an alleyway – or one of so many ephemeral moments that were somehow not ephemeral at all because, drunk on autumn, he felt as if the history of the world were being collected. He could almost hear the scratchy nibs of ancient pens recording everything. When he was a child he used to ask questions such as: How many ants are there in the whole world? Or: Who is the cleverest person in the world? And the point of the question was not to know the answer but the strange thrill in believing someone or something did know. As a child he had never needed to know the answer. But somehow, somewhere along the way, he had needed to know. Urgently. As if his life had depended upon it.

***

He saw her again at Godrevy, from a distance. She was lugging her great box around, leaning into windows, chatting to customers. He knew he wanted her but he did not want to want her. He watched her come closer to the parked cars near his van. He watched her black hair catch the sunlight and turn blue, and her wide, white smile that made deep lines in her cheeks. She seemed something so precious, so unquantifiably precious he could almost believe in her. He brought his hand to his mouth to ponder this approaching credulity and it felt good to have his hand there. He realised he was licking his finger and his finger was sweet. A good, fruity, musty sweet. He looked down and saw a dribble of ice-cream at the edge of a tub of blueberry burst. He smiled and remembered their first meeting, and his joke about blueberry gloom. It seemed impossibly long ago, something fading fast. He felt the need to share the memory with her. He got out of the van and approached her.

'I tasted your blueberry burst,' he said. 'And this time it was rather nice.'

'Good,' she said, She was at the window of a car, serving a customer.

'Do you remember the day we met?' he said.

And he felt that day now, in the telling. And that grey, blowy March afternoon was becoming more than it ever was and he knew it, but he didn't care because he felt something real in it despite the facts. He saw it now: golden and sunny. Like autumn. It made him feel warm inside.

She finished serving her customer, dropped her bucket and looked at him.

'Do you remember what I called your blueberry ice-cream?' he said.

She made a big show of trying to remember, looking up at the sky off to one side.

'I called it blueberry gloom,' he said.

'So you did,' she said. She picked up her bucket. 'It's been a long day.'

Henry walked back to the van. 'Blueberry gloom,' he said to himself. He got back in and watched her pack her things in her car. And the sky above deepened and husbands and wives opened doors and splashed Thermos dregs on to the damp grass and engines coughed to life as all the world went home for dinner. And she went home too, her muddy car rattling along the rough track as she headed towards Hayle.

***

On the last day of October, he came. A bright sunny morning, it was. And as the little van dipped and bucked across the grass car park, one could feel the chill of November in the air and see it in the frosty patches of shaded ground under hedges. Henry stopped in a far corner of the car park and opened his window.

A blast of broken Greensleeves filled the air. Naive children, the kind who smiled at anything that was bright and shiny and tinkles, and who did not know broken glass from precious gems, gave longing looks to parents.

One child approached, and the cool dew snapped at his little ankles as he crossed the field. Cows watched him come, masticating not stupidly at all, but with a seen-it-all-before nonchalance of creatures well-acquainted with Henry's work.

'And how,' said Henry, 'might I help you, young man?'

The child looked at the menu. A single, vanilla ice-cream stared back. He looked at Henry then back at the board. Something was wrong, but he didn't know what.

'A 99, please.'

Henry dropped his hands on to the counter and leaned out of his hatch. 'I am completely out of vanilla ice-cream.'

The child backed away. He looked at the board again, then back to Henry. 'What else have you got?'

'Nothing,' said Henry. 'Absolutely nothing at all.'

The young man continued to look from Henry to the board. There was nothing more to be done, but he didn't seem to want to go. And Henry seemed disinclined to let him go. The child shifted from foot to foot. Henry cleared his throat and then peered out of the hatch at a cow pissing in an adjacent field. After a along while, the cow finished pissing. 'Remarkable,' said Henry and leaned back in.

'Still here?' he said to the child. 'You'd best be on your way.'

The child took a last longing look at the vanilla ice-cream, turned and began to trudge away.

'Unless...' said Henry.

The boy stopped and turned around.

'... this is of any use to you.'

And there in Henry Caldwell's outstretched hand – it seemed he would hold it as far away from himself as he could – was a thing the likes of which had surely never been seen at Godrevy or beyond. Towering above a frail sugar cone, sat a great clot of ice-cream in no one particular colour but rather every colour imaginable. And yet the ice-cream, magnificently garish as it was, played only a supporting role to the various appendages that decorated it: bits of flake, Smarties, chocolate drops and other sweets clinging to the icy surface like limpets to a rock.

'Wow,' said the child. 'What's it called?'

Henry pointed a finger at the child. 'A good question, young man. It's a 114.'

'How much is it?'

'Are you paying cash?'

The child nodded. Henry handed the boy the ice-cream. 'Nothing for cash' The child grinned and walked away, brandishing his ice-cream like a torch above his head one minute and licking it the next. In a moment, two more children arrived. Then, before Henry had even finished serving, four more. Within half an hour that little corner thronged with children, and even the cows in the adjacent field crowded together and peered over the hedge to watch the commotion.

'Here's something I thought I'd never see.'

Henry looked up from the fridge. Sarah stood at the hatch. He handed her an ice-cream.

'What's it called?' she said.

'It's a 114.'

'Oh Christ,' she said.

She shook her head, turned around and started to walk away. Her shoulders began to shake with laughter. Henry watched her as she went, her flakes wobbling and Smarties loosening and falling off the ice-cream into the grass. He continued handing out his garish ice-creams, scaring the children a little with his complicated questions and headmasterly tones. 'We needn't worry,' he said, 'that a 99 is not made of 99 separate parts. It is merely our starting point, our number one if you will. And it is the 15 additional flavours and appendages that bring us to our magic number.'

He watched her walk away. She turned around to look at him. 'And there is, admittedly, a little magic in it,' he said. And he felt something travelling up the back of his spine. It was as cold as ice-cream and yet left him warm and clammy in the face and fingers. He felt full of a mess of emotions, felt overwhelmed, in fact, as he dipped his head into the bowels of his freezer and scooped up another dollop.

old broken window bachelor

PEOPLE ASKED him why he didn't replace the window and Archie just shrugged.

'I haven't really thought about it,' he said.

'But Archie, boy, it will let the cold in and to be perfectly honest it doesn't look right, a house on Queen's Way all falling down next door to Sandra Eddie's with her lovely bit of turquoise woodwork on the window frames and her knick-knacks on the sills.'

Archie just shrugged.

But it made him sad. These boys in the pub badgering him: once they were big strong men who would fill your face in if you looked at them wrong. Now they were laying in their beds at night worrying about Archie's windows. All the world had gone to shit. All of them were fading away. They had their moment as young men. Jesus Christ, Archie could see them now laughing and joking with fags in their hands. Their strong, hard arms. Yet now they spent their days mincing their words and apologising and walking with humility as if paying for the crimes of their younger selves. Like once they were made of gold and now they are made of sand. Archie hardly recognised them any more. Men he was scared of as a youngster averted their eyes when he shambled into the pub.

All the world had gone to shit.

They admired him though. Occasionally they would look at him with jealous eyes, as if they wished they had his freedom. But it was just the ghost of their younger selves looking. In truth they shivered at the thought of his bachelor's life, with his broken window, his mop of thick yellow hair – how is Archie's hair still blond? – his plastic bag and his suit harbouring stale smoke from the 1950s. And they said to their wives, 'I saw Archie earlier.' And their wives tutted and the men shook their heads and smiled and said, 'Poor old boy. Who would have thought Archie would end up like that? It's not much life for a man.'

***

Archie had a wonderful life. He got up when he wanted to – usually after three or four fags and after the kids had walked past on their way to school. Then he pushed his forearm over the breakfast table in a clatter of old cutlery and jam pots to make room and ate some Sugar Puffs. He listened to the radio as he ate, and listened to the trains clatter by his little house, but mainly he spent his time thinking about what to do with his day before it was decent to go to the pub.

Then he walked to The Plantation, North Quay or Memorial Walk, sat down and smoked a few fags. He liked places with plenty of space. He squinted, smoked and thought about the bigger picture. A man can get so caught up with emulsion paint and windows and polishing the car when the real world is out there, in the spaces between things. Where the wind gusts and the seagulls skid and shriek across the sky. A man must be where his thoughts might soar, not staring at the little bits and pieces of the world so hard he doesn't see that they are just brush strokes for the bigger picture.

Archie loved Hayle. He loved its faded glory. And while councillors wet themselves as they shook hands with the next batch of developers who proposed 2,000 little white boxes along the crumbling harbour, so that

Hayle could be grown up and sensible and like one of those sketches architects make with block-paved streets and women pushing prams, the town went on as ever. With its faraway looks over rubble towards the beach and the bay, its seagulls high above, screeching distant, impractical thoughts. The town was like a wonderful overlong youth, frayed and worn in places (most places) but somehow youthful all the same. It was a dream world. And yet it was real. And the so-called real, sensible world: it languished in architectural plans and in the minds of councillors. Hayle was a little anomaly of purity. Just like Archie with his fags and his poetic thoughts and his pub and the long, uncompromised life he had never betrayed.

He was lonely. Just like Hayle was lonely as the wind whipped along North Quay and bent wild flowers to the dirt. But it was life as he had promised to live it.

***

One day forty years earlier, Archie sat on the dunes with Richard Berryman. They were partners in crime. All of life was about beer and women and novels and poetry. They sat there with their sunsets and their rippling ocean, marvelling that this life was so wonderful and yet so few people knew about it. It made them shout at houses in the night. Literally. They got drunk and screamed at windows, and told the people beyond about the silver sky and the bats that flickered. They scoffed and laughed at people who did not come to the dunes to drink beer and watch the sunset.

They were rare men, not realising that Hayle was full of rare men and women who turned their backs on beauty because they believed if they kept looking at it through their twenties and into their thirties it would drive them mad. Archie and Richard did not know about all that yet.

Richard was getting drunk. He looked at the sun setting out in the ocean and pointed at it and said, 'That is what I want. That out there. And I am going to have it.' And he said it solemnly as if he knew already that the path he was choosing would be a difficult one, with many temptations on the way.

Archie admired him immensely. Richard had black eyes, thick black hair and a jutting chin. He looked as if he were arrogantly challenging the world.

And Archie knew what he meant as he looked at that sunset.

'Beauty, always beauty,' said Archie. 'Even if we must sink to our knees to have it.'

It was a vague interchange, but the lager made the words soar in their minds. It contained everything that needed to be said. It was a seminal moment. A manifesto.

Richard was married within 12 months to a woman he didn't love. He said something about youth burning out in the end. It was poetic in its way, but it had the stale whiff of cliche about it. Like the rest of his life did. And he didn't look Archie in the eye when he said it.

That was the start. Other men followed. Once they shambled about together in mismatched clothes, borrowing others' jackets and jumpers, loitering in Foundry Square like scarecrows. They got wives and smartened up. They dressed in shades that matched their new homes. They faded away in well-presented rooms with soft furnishings.

***

Archie spent a lot of time in the White Hart. The old boys were always the same, but every year or two a new batch of youngsters came tumbling through the door. Young women sat by the fire and crossed their legs and rolled their fags and chatted to Archie and became his friend. They said things like, 'Awww you're so sweet I love you, Archie.' They drank cider and black and said 'fucking' the way young girls do nowadays: well enunciated, slightly posh, using it to bring some heat to any subject – poetry, politics, animal rights, vegetarianism – they had a heart for. Occasionally they got thrown out for swearing and being too drunk. They were intelligent, passionate young women.

Then they would disappear. Archie might see them three or four years later, with a well-turned-out boy. They would come in and poke their head around the door, nervous, as if they might find their former selves in there ready to pin them to the wall and give them hell. They ordered drinks like mice, apologised when they got their change and sat with their boy, leaning in and whispering at him earnestly. Occasionally they would see Archie sitting by the fire and say 'Hi, Archie' – they never called him Old Cock Face any more – and 'Oh my God' as if it was incredible he was sitting there just as he had done all those years ago (three years ago). Then they would spend the rest of the evening avoiding his eye. When they left he rarely saw them again. If he did he'd see these once wild, swearing, swaying young woman hurrying in and out of shiny cars in Foundry Square and rushing into shops with perturbed looks, as if they'd been in earlier and had left something expensive on the counter.

One might believe that the brief, wild youth was merely a role. Archie knew the truth. The women they had become was the role. A big part it was, with a lot of lines to learn. A hell of a performance.

***

One day he met a young woman in the White Hart. She was called Angela. She was a small thing with glossy blonde hair and a top lip so full and brimming looking at it made Archie feel weak. So he tried not to look. When he talked to her he stared past her or at his pint, or at the end of his burning fag. He stole glimpses at her the way you steal glimpses at a setting sun.

They sat in the pub one spring evening, by the open fire. She asked him why he'd never got married. For once, Archie held her gaze. 'Because I never fell in love,' he said. 'Most of them got married and most of them weren't in love. You won't understand it now, my love, but a man gets to a certain age and the world he thought was so big and beautiful gets too big for him. That's the moment a man gets married. Not because he's in love. At least, not very often.'

And Archie said all this quietly, leaning forward so Angela could hear and the men at the bar couldn't.

'You're saying you never met the right girl?'

'That's it,' said Archie.

She was the wildest one of them all. One night they were knocking them back, Archie on the bitter, Angela on vodka. She had this sparkle, this light, in her eyes when she was drunk. Something dangerous. It got into you, it invaded you, like the flash from a camera does. Men at the bar couldn't stop looking at her in her short skirt. But she stared back and they looked away. There was such youthful arrogance in those flashing eyes. The light got deep inside. It challenged you. Made you feel inadequate, guilty. Even big men like Barry Harbollow shrank before those eyes, as if they finally understood the waste and lies of their lives.

She got louder and louder, her voice more high pitched the drunker she got. She got into an argument about politics with the cronies at the bar. She stumbled into a chair and knocked it over. She was a total pain in the arse. Even Archie knew it. Then she drew a swastika on the dartboard.

'That it,' said Tina behind the bar. 'Get out. And you, Archie, you're old enough to know better. Making a fool of yourself over a girl.'

***

In the mornings, before they went to the pub, they walked around Hayle. When he'd been hungover and walking with a woman in the past, Archie had felt like the world was wrapped in cellophane. Now, as they crunched through the rubble and dry ferns of North Quay, it felt as wide and wild as usual. He talked and talked, pointing out things on the quay, the dunes and the beach, as if he were verbalising the accumulated thoughts of 40-odd years.

On the beach, the wind blew her hair over her face. She had this way of pulling strands across her forehead and behind her ear when she asked important questions. Then she'd hold them there while she waited for Archie's reply, frowning into the sand.

She said things like, 'Why do people spend a lifetime doing jobs they hate? Don't they realise life is so short? Don't they ever walk through a graveyard or see an old person and think, fuck I'd better sort it out quick, live the way I want to because I'm going to die?'

They were naive questions, but they got to the heart of things. Archie realised there was a wisdom in that naivety, an essential truth beyond all the clutter and junk of experience.

'What you are is what I am and what I've been trying to hold on to all my life,' said Archie one morning. He thought she wouldn't understand, but she did. She

119

looked at him with those eyes, those lips, and nodded and said, 'I know, Archie.'

Then she said, 'Shall we go to the pub?' Archie laughed and she squeezed his hand and let go.

It was a wonderful thing to be in the Copperhouse at lunchtime. They sat at a table by the window and rolled their fags and drank their pints. Fugitives from the shithole world. People passed back and forth on the pavement. 'They look into the pub, some of them, as if they would love to give up the whole thing,' said Archie. 'Give it all up, step inside, roll a fag and have a drink. But they don't because the thought is with them only for a second and then they've passed the window and the thought is gone.' He was exuberant and chuckling when he began this observation, but by the time he'd finished there was something ugly in his voice. A jeery tone.

They went back to Archie's house mid afternoon, for a bite to eat and a cup of tea before they went out in the evening. It was the first time Angela had been to Archie's house. 'It's beautiful,' she said, standing as Archie moved stacks of newspapers from the sofa so she could sit down. He made coffee. He gave her the crappiest, chipped and stained cup he could find. He told her so as she drank and she laughed and Archie laughed and his spirits lifted again. It was a good feeling, that afternoon, slowly sobering up as the sunlight streamed in. The fag smoke pearling in beams of light. The goosebumps on Angela's white thighs. The way she sat there, smiling, her knees together, stealing glimpses at the squalor. The sound of the train clattering by, people going to and fro with their lives, between their lives, as they sat together in a perfect moment. He remembered how they slowly shifted from an alcohol to a caffeine buzz, from hazy golden truths to urgent ones, saying I know I know at what the other had to say about politicians and Hayle and the way some people crippled themselves financially to drive big cars.

Before they went out he said, 'Angela, I'm being serious now. Deadly serious. Never marry a man unless you love him.'

'I won't,' she said. 'I couldn't.'

'What I mean to say,' said Archie, 'is that life isn't so bad if you don't.'

'I know,' she said.

'You don't have to marry at all,' he said.

'I know,' she said.

***

At the end of the summer, Angela went away to university. She said she would see him at Christmas and Archie said, 'Yeah yeah, I'll see you at Christmas.' He tried to say it as if he didn't believe she would come back to him and as if he didn't care one way or the other. He tried to believe that for a day or two, but one morning he took his walk across North Quay and he just couldn't see it any more. The rubble, the weeds, the lobster pots, the swirling waters – all of it was a sham. It was like looking at something that had happened already, something that was over.

He went back to the White Hart. People said, 'where's your young lady' and Archie said 'I don't need no young lady'.

Tina from behind the bar came and sat with him. 'It's dangerous, Archie,' she said. 'Youth like that. It'll tear you apart. It'll tear you apart,' she said again. She looked serious. Her fag pointed towards the ceiling. She sighed and her top lip, so flaccid and wrinkled, flapped and vibrated. It seemed people knew of the dangers of flirting with youth. They talked about it wisely. Poetically. With great pleasure. It was good to know you had no choice. It was good to know it would tear you apart.

Afterwards the boys at the bar growled and spoke lewdly about Angela's legs. Archie remembered how scared of her they had been. How they would never have spoken like this if she had been here. It made him proud of her.

That evening, Archie walked around the Weir. The days were pulling in. The water swirled. Small figures hit golf balls over the river on the links at Lelant. As the land got darker the sky seemed to get brighter. It was full of blue and pink and orange. Archie walked around the Weir. Then he walked around again until he could barely see his feet. Then he went up to the Standard, sat in the corner and drank five pints of bitter. It was quiet. The kids that were left, those that didn't go to university, were playing the quiz machine. You could hear the ones that were gone, answering the questions.

***

In December he noticed some of the kids had come back from university. They were back in the White Hart. They marvelled at the pool table with the chipped balls, the juke box that played vinyl and the old-fashioned furnishings. They praised everything.

Archie got into an argument with a tall, red-haired young man who sat next to him on the sofa by the fire. The young man smiled and looked about him as if he was greatly amused. 'You act as if you've been away ten years, not ten minutes,' said Archie.

'Ten weeks,' said the young man.

'Ten minutes, ten weeks,' said Archie. 'It's nothing.'

It was the kind of thing an old man said.

On Christmas Day he was tilting a bowl up to his

mouth, drinking the sweet milk from his Sugar Puffs, when someone knocked the door. He lowered the bowl and saw Angela's form rippling through the glass. He got up, opened the door, turned around and walked inside. She came in. Archie turned and looked at her. They said nothing. Angela was smiling. She walked up to him.

'Merry Christmas, you old bastard,' she said, and she wrapped her arms around him and buried her head on his chest. He felt her hair catch in his bristly chin.

They walked over North Quay, up the hill past Electric Works and on to the dunes, each clasping a bottle of sherry. From time to time they walked through holiday parks.

'This one's like a concentration camp,' said Angela. 'The kind of place they house people before they kill them. Look, there are even signs with great big alsatians on them. What kind of people build a concentration camp on the dunes? And use alsations to threaten local people to keep away? Cunts.'

They walked on and reached Gwithian Towans. It was beautiful here. Decaying breeze block buildings littered the dunes. The buildings weren't ugly.

'The dunes have reclaimed them,' said Angela, lingering on the word reclaimed in a languorous, mock-pretentious voice.

A cold wind blew, so they stepped inside one of the buildings. It had no roof and no windows, but it kept out the wind. They sat opposite each other, their bums on breeze blocks, their feet on grass, and drank the sherry. Archie asked Angela how university was and she said it was fine. They drank quickly to warm themselves. Archie got drunk and the fool in him felt Angela was looking at him a certain way. Those eyes flickered, almost crackled. Her plump upper lip broke his heart. He heard himself speaking before he even had time to think

'It's a bastard thing,' he said. 'A bastard thing. I was right all along. I knew I was right.' He took a long slug of the sherry. 'I waited and waited. But it's too late. A good thirty years too late.'

Grass and breeze block and clouds broke up before his eyes. He wiped his eyes. Angela, her knees touching, looked at him and smiled. Then suddenly she shivered and took a long gulp from her bottle.

They finished the sherry, walked through the concentration camp and had three or four in the Bucket of Blood. They were both very drunk now. They spent a lot of time smoking fags and blowing noisily. It was a kind of conversation, that smoke blowing. They also did things with their cigarettes like roll the tips against the edge of the ashtray to peel away the crusty layer of grey and reveal the burning orange, or tap them when they didn't need tapping.

***

Archie woke up in the night. The TV flickered.

'It's cold, Archie,' said Angela. 'Really cold.'

He took off his coat and covered her. He patted it down over her shoulders. Then he tucked it in, making sure bits of the coat were wedged between her shoulder blades and the settee, so no cold air could get at her.

He woke up two or three times in the night. The TV lit the room, but only with a grey flicker that made it impossible for him to tell if she was sleeping or awake.

He woke up in the morning. Light came in the windows. She was sitting opposite him, still wrapped up in the coat, smiling.

'Boxing Day,' she said.

Archie got up and put the coffee on. He found her a nice mug.

When he gave her the coffee, she said, 'Archie, for fuck's sake fix that broken window.'

'I will,' he said.

They talked for a bit about what families do at Christmas. They joked about how they got sick of each other all cooped up, but forced themselves to be together, like they thought it would be a sin to go and see their mates and have a pint. Then Angela said she had to go. They stood in the doorway. She beckoned Archie with her finger and she kissed him on the cheek. He felt those soft lips on his stubbly face. He imagined how his stubbly face would feel against those lips.

Then Angela was walking away. She turned and waved. Then she turned the corner and disappeared. Archie looked at the places she had been a moment before, then he looked up at the sky. It was a beautiful day. A beautiful, blue day. A clean day. Archie put on a fresh shirt and went to the White Hart.

the stroke of the tongue

AS 18-YEAR-OLD Hayle Carnival Queen Noreen Penglaze waved at the crowds on July 12 1937, she had no inkling that this would be the happiest moment of her life. How could she? There were many years yet to come – sixty to be precise – with which to compare that unusually warm and joyful occasion. There was also that hateful human phenomenon of never quite knowing what a truly happy occasion is until it has passed, and one must look back at a joyous time with the memory flickering and guttering now in a winter of frigid disappointments.

But, as she waved in her white, diaphanous gloves, she did sense that today was the beginning of something. Which was true. When she looked back many years later, however, she decided that the moment was more noteworthy in terms of endings. And that was true, too.

Noreen was an innocent young woman. The kind who, according to her father, could walk through shit and come out with the hems of her dress as white as snow. And there was plenty of shit around, because Father was a milkman and Noreen was often in the garden feeding the old carthorse posies of grass and flowers as the old beast farted and dropped more manure than even the most enthusiastic vegetable gardener could cope with. Somehow she floated like an angel above that dung-mined terrain, her milky gaze delighting in the beauty of the sky and the birds as her feet followed their own happy course through a maze of excrement.

'It's all an act,' said Mother. 'She's got airs.'

And it was a source of annoyance to Mother that a

child brought up with seven brothers and sisters in a cramped terraced cottage – an abode where bathing, evacuations and other necessities were carried out in such close proximity to one's family – should be so refined in sensibility. Father said she would grow up soon and discover that life for the working man and woman was essentially hard and miserable. And that was at least some comfort to Mother.

There were few clouds to darken Noreen's youth, but one arrived on Carnival Day in 1937; on that very same day Noreen experienced the happiest moment of her life. The cloud was Maggie Bern, a black-haired girl with dark-brown eyes and a womanly figure who seemed to outshine even Noreen. At least from several yards. But on closer examination the consensus was that she lost out to Noreen on account of the spongy wide pores of her face and, most particularly, the unladylike black moustache that grew first at the far edges of her top lip but, as the seasons passed, threatened to meet authentically in the middle. The moustache would have sat more comfortably on a plain girl, and blended more with a general state of uncomeliness. In Maggie's case it was a corrupting influence, a furry reminder every time she ran her tongue over her top lip that she was a slither, a hair's breadth, as it were, from genuine beauty. She shaved the moustache and soon the lip-licking became a bristly reminder, pricking her tongue and deflating her confidence in the presence of men. How odd that the boys saw this nervous habit as the lewdest flirtation in all of Hayle.

By the time she was 18 and Noreen was Hayle Carnival Queen, Maggie had fully realised the powers of her lip-licking, and had felt more pricks than the bristly ones on her tongue as a consequence. She accommodated 13 young men in Hayle and had a flagrant future ahead. She felt no shame, but she did feel lonely in her liberation. And she combated that loneliness by accusing anyone in her vicinity – particularly the girls – of the lewdest behaviour.

'I seen you last night, Edith Parker – pulling down your drawers up Burntcottagelane for Jack Kernick. Arse showing like a great full moon.'

'I never did,' said Edith.

But it was said and Maggie felt better.

'And you, Vera Dolly. You had no knickers on at the pictures and George Rose had his hand right up between your legs.'

If a stranger came to Hayle and was accosted by Maggie, he would surely believe himself in Cornwall's very own Gomorrah, a town trembling around the thighs and panting in the frosty night air.

Noreen didn't feature much in Maggie's bawdy fantasies. Maggie had tried to include her once or twice, but this ethereal being walked through the writhing tableaux untouched, her chilly innocence draining the life out of the innuendoes. At least it did until the appearance of Richard Canker on Carnival Day in 1937. His arrival inspired Maggie to conjure stories about Noreen more depraved than anything that had come before.

And why was Maggie inspired to initiate her lewdest fantasies yet on Carnival Day in 1937? Because on this very day she took quite a fancy to Richard. And Richard, meanwhile, was taking quite a fancy to Carnival Queen Noreen Penglaze.

***

'You're new around here,' said Maggie. 'Two weeks,' said Richard. 'I haven't been out much yet.'

'Where you from?'

'Camborne.'

Maggie nodded as if that explained everything.

'People don't just move to Hayle. I expect you were playing around in your best pal's fiance's knickers.'

Richard shook his head solemnly. 'I've got a job at the furniture workshop.'

'You might have a job, but that doesn't hide the fact you were caught with one hand on her boobs and the other in her drawers. So you had to leave, see.'

'I see,' said Richard, smiling.

Maggie turned to the crowd behind her and caught Sally Pellow's eye.

'This chap here is new in Hayle. He had to leave Camborne because he was playing around in his best friend's fiance's drawers.'

'The dirty sod,' said Sally.

'Hang on a minute,' said Richard. 'That's a lie. I never put my hand in any girl's drawers, let alone my best friend's fiance's.'

'So your best friend does have a fiance?' said Maggie.

'As a matter of fact, he does.'

'There you go, Sally,' said Maggie. 'You can deny what you want, but the evidence speaks for itself.'

The pair giggled away. Richard shrugged. He was a good-looking man in shades of brown: dark brown hair, hazel eyes, a light brown beard. He looked like a solid, steady fellow who would grow roots wherever he should settle. The kind of man who could endure a torrent of Maggie's wicked talk and come out unscathed, and good.

Maggie liked him.

'So are you going to take me out?' she said.

'You're a bold one.'

'There's no harm in asking.'

She smiled at Richard. The sun shone on her glossy hair; she tucked a stray lock behind her ear. Richard smiled back at her.

'I don't know,' he said. 'This is all a bit fast for me.'

'Fast? This is as slow as an old nag on the road to the knacker's yard.' Maggie threw back her head and laughed, her mouth wide, her furry tongue trembling. Richard didn't laugh; he watched her. He seemed attracted and repelled by her at the same time. Maggie flashed a glance at him as she recovered from her convulsions. She squeezed her fists and frowned as she looked at this slim, solid, brown man. She was embarrassed. And then he wasn't looking at her anymore.

Maggie turned and saw the object of his unflickering gaze: Noreen Penglaze on horse and cart, waving a white-gloved hand to the crowds below, her golden blonde hair pulled back from her face to reveal pale, translucent features brushed with veiny blue. A face that could fade away from improbable delicateness if it weren't for those big blue eyes. Her lips were a little pursed, as if too much smile would be unseemly, and she waved with limp regality, but those eyes bravely held the gaze of the townsfolk and were full of happiness and pride. It was the kind of beauty that made one frown, as if it took an act of concentration to keep it there, to stop it from fading away.

Richard Canker followed her progress as she floated by, his top lip disappearing inside his mouth as his words and thoughts turned inwards. Beauty such as this gave a man a lot to think about.

Maggie hung on to Richard as the crowds dispersed and the pair, along with Sally Pellow, walked back to Foundry Square and mingled outside the bakery. A few others lingered around, not quite ready to go home, but not quite sure how to continue entertaining themselves after the carnival.

Things livened up a bit with the arrival of masters Dick Elliot and Arthur Tredinnick. They came out of the shadows of the viaduct, convulsions of laughter announcing their appearance in the pinkish evening light, Arthur slapping Dick on the back, the latter lurching forward and then stopping, holding his hands on his knees as he hooted with mirth. Smiles grew on faces as the pair took their places on the steps of the bakery, lit their Woodbines and then proceeded to entertain the crowd by mimicking the conversations of Hayle's few dignitaries.

Maggie, Richard and Sally watched. The girls giggled and Richard smoked, the orange glow of his cigarette growing brighter as the evening drew in.

Arthur and Dick had loosened up the crowd and were approaching full flow when a solitary figure floated into view.

'There she is,' said Dick. 'Noreen Penglaze, Hayle Carnival Queen 1937.'

The crowd turned to look at Noreen in her white, diaphanous regalia. She seemed translucent under gaslight.

'What are you doing walking home on your own?' said Arthur.

'Mother and Father are still in the Standard,' said Noreen.

The crowd was silent for a moment, watching.

'Father likes a drink, doesn't he?' said Arthur.

'From time to time,' said Noreen.

'Well, you walk home safely, my lover. And watch out for Mayor Hartley. They say he has taken quite a fancy to you today.'

The crowd chuckled and turned back to Dick and

Arthur. But both were sucking on their Woodbines in respectful silence. Heads turned back towards the gaslight again.

Noreen hadn't moved. There was an awkward silence.

Then Dick said, 'Hey, what are we thinking of? Three cheers for the Carnival Queen! Hip Hip!'

'Hooray.'

Noreen smiled as they cheered, clutching her hands in front of her. And yet when they finished still she didn't go. The crowd murmured. People grew impatient. Maggie watched Richard's dark eyes flash glances at Noreen.

'I'll tell you why she was chosen to be this year's carnival queen,' she said, addressing the crowd.

Richard turned to look at Maggie, his expression darkening at this ruddy intrusion into a realm of ghostly beauty. Maggie winked at him.

'She sucked Mayor Hartley's thing up the institute.'

Silence.

'God's truth,' she added. 'Either that or his zipper got caught in his trousers. And Noreen was good enough to get on her knees and help him out.'

Still silence. Faces glared at Maggie, then looked at Noreen, a brittle moth under lamplight. Maggie gripped Richard's arm. Things were in the balance; it seemed no one knew quite what to do. Until a snort of laughter from someone trying – but failing – to repress their mirth tipped the scales; and the thought of defending the honour of young Noreen Penglaze rapidly gave way to great hoots of laughter as the crowd relieved themselves of all that repressed hilarity.

Richard didn't laugh. He detached Maggie's claw from his arm – she was hanging on to him as she convulsed with the rest of them – sidled through the crowd, took Noreen by the arm and led her out of the light and away from the laughter. The mirth died away as the crowd watched them go.

'She'll be sucking his thing next,' said Maggie.

They all laughed again. But not as heartily this time. And Maggie didn't laugh at all. She was licking her lips and feeling the pricks of her stubbly moustache. And thinking.

***

Some people say that idealists become the greatest cynics when they learn what the world is really all about. It's a fate to be wished on no one, but one that Noreen was destined to suffer. But what about idealists who remain idealists, despite what the world has to teach them? They become tyrants. And that was the fate of Richard. And it made a misery of Noreen's life for all the time they spent together.

Maggie's gossip brought the pair closer together. It was soon apparent – to everyone but Noreen and Richard – that after they had consummated their passion in Parson Rosewarne's stables, their sexual shenanigans became increasingly flagrant. Maggie had seen them trembling in the night at no less than five different locations, the fifth alleged sighting – in the entranceway to Higgledy Haberdashery – backed up by a pair of greasy handprints pressed on the glass. Maggie explained the significance of the handprints to those a bit slow on the uptake, even leaning against Higgledy's herself and pushing her arse in the air. Hooter Davey said the prints were too big to be a woman's hands. Ethel Simmons illustrated the error in Hooter's thinking by pointing out that Maggie's hands fitted perfectly over the prints. Hooter thought for a moment and said that

Noreen's hands certainly weren't as big as Maggie's, but the matter was briskly brought to a close by Maggie, who removed her hands from the pane and shifted the conversation on to some general observations about the couple's behaviour.

'Dirty buggers,' she said.

Hooter and Ethel agreed despite the lack of solid evidence, and thereby illustrated a tendency common among Hayle people to believe something shocking rather than doubt it, because it gave one something to get one's teeth into and talk about.

All of the time Noreen and Richard were apparently sweating and thrusting their way around Hayle, they were, in fact, hiding themselves away from the gossiping Maggie in Mr and Mrs Penglaze's kitchen, discussing the merits of The Socialist Medical Association. Or at least Richard was talking and the others were listening with as much politeness as they could muster.

'Free health care for all is the first step,' said Richard, warming his hands on the stove. 'Then will come equal wages for every man, regardless of his vocation.'

'I shan't need no health care,' said Mr Penglaze. 'When my time comes I shall just drop dead, like my father and his father before him.'

'But many people will benefit,' said Richard.

'I shan't know either way if I'm dead, shall I?' said Father, smiling and raising his voice at Richard's illogical reasoning.

There were many conversations along these lines between Richard and Mr Penglaze, two lines of thought never quite meeting, either in agreement or in disagreement. There was a hint of bloody mindedness in Mr Penglaze's failure to connect with Richard. And humour, too. It was all a bit of sly fun, though Richard, of course, would never know it. Despite a healthy interest in the politics of the day, he was not a self-aware man.

'I would say he's as daft as a brush,' said Father. 'Although that wouldn't be quite fair on the brush, because at least that's useful for something.'

Richard's colleagues at the furniture workshop agreed. He had quickly become popular among the men, who took no end of delight in making fun of him while still retaining his complete confidence and good humour. This delicate art was immortalised in a photo taken by George Armstrong, the sepia snap a treasure that brought delight to scores of visitors – young and old – to the Armstrong household in the years to come.

In the photo, Richard gritted his teeth with exertion and grinned into the camera, a lick of hair falling over his face, his chin and beard jutting forth. And the reason for all this hard work? Richard had a plank of wood on his shoulders which was connected, by a chain at either end, to a pair of buckets. Richard's feet were in the buckets and he strained against the wood with all his might. On either side of him were George Thursday and Albert Taskis, bending their legs and encouraging Richard, each with one sly eye on the camera.

'Go on, boy. Yes, that's it! You're off the bloody ground!'

Poor Richard. Such was his optimism at the potential of man. And while George and Albert knew nothing of Newton's third law of motion with its equal and opposite reaction, they did know a thing or two about common sense; something Richard was no more likely to possess, no matter how he sweated and grunted, than he was to float in thin air.

***

Richard and Noreen married in July 1938, almost a year to the day after their first meeting.

Within months of the marriage Noreen fell to earth, and was all the better for it. This Richard Canker with his woody hues and honest beard was a living, breathing man who had awful breath first thing; and he ate his food in a fussy and unmanly way, too, consuming his vegetables and potatoes first before moving on to the meat.

Noreen was disappointed. The girl in her faded away. Her flesh lost that papery sheen and thickened, taking on the ruddy hue of the busy housewife; and she laughed a little deeper at innuendoes she had merely tinkled at uncomprehendingly before. She was becoming a woman. A good woman. It was a shame Richard didn't see it that way.

To be fair to Richard he had high standards, based on a vision he had fostered since the age of 15. It was a scanty kind of vision, not fleshed out, as it were. In it a woman – very much like a pre-nuptials Noreen – sat at a kitchen table and nodded with glassy eyes as he banged the table in indignation at the lot of the working man. Finally, this ghostly woman shed a tear at his nobility as he continued his impassioned speech.

That was it. A mere sketch of the woman who would make him happy. If only Richard had realised Noreen was the woman in his little daydream, and that she had merely fleshed out the character for occasions when something other than rapt adoration was required, his life may have taken a different turn. As it was he interpreted his corporeal wife as all too of this flesh. The crackle of a brush through her hair, the brisk and over-efficient swishing sound her skirts made as she moved around the kitchen, and that regrettable (tut tut) trait of lightly repeating air through her windpipe when she ate: all these things were not compatible with his idea of womanhood.

All came to a head one January morning. Noreen was sweeping in the kitchen, looking a little blowsy and harassed, strands of hair escaping her bun and falling like gossamer threads on her shoulders. Richard sat at the table eating a slice of dry bread as he looked over the paper.

'Have you seen the dustpan, Richard?' said Noreen.

Richard chewed, and finished the column he was reading.

'Where did we agree it should live, Noreen?'

'In the cupboard under the sink.'

'Have you looked in the cupboard under the sink, Noreen?'

'I didn't... I thought... No, I haven't.'

'In that case, I should have a look in the cupboard under the sink, Noreen.'

Richard turned the page, shook it smooth and continued reading, masticating his bread so thoroughly it began to turn sweet in his mouth. Noreen bent down, opened the cupboard and then peered inside.

A sharp rattle broke the silence. Richard swallowed the sweet pulp and stiffened, his eyes boring through words.

Noreen straightened up, cleared her throat and began to hum a tune, but it quickly petered out. Richard tried to focus on the words in the paper. It was no good. Silence descended. Her fart had ripped a hole in the brittle space inhabited by the newly married pair. All sound, motion and hope seemed to rush towards and disappear into that flatulent gap, leaving Richard and Noreen in empty space.

Richard folded up his newspaper, scraped back his chair and stood up.

'I think I'll go out and stretch my legs,' he said.

'But it's raining,' said Noreen.

'Never mind. A bit of fresh air will do me good.'

***

Richard didn't speak to Noreen for three days. All conjugal relations were suspended indefinitely. It was a tragedy for Noreen. She was a young woman coming to terms with the compromises of the world, delighting in the more rounded, colloquial tones she spoke in, feeling more of this Cornish earth and taking great pleasure in the thrill of intercourse with a sweating man who scratched her chin red with his rough beard.

On the fourth day, Richard said, 'As much as it pains me, Noreen, I must ask you a question, and I require an honest answer.'

'Anything,' said Noreen, patting her wet hands on her apron, dragging a chair up next to him and sitting down.

Richard held her hands in his and looked into her eyes.

'Did you do anything with Mayor Hartley?'

'No!' said Noreen. 'Never.'

'Do you promise?'

'I do!'

'Then why did you look away from me for a moment?'

'I didn't.'

'What are you hiding from me, Noreen?'

'Nothing!'

'Then why did that girl say such things about you?'

'Maggie Bern says wicked things about everyone.'

'Then why does the damn thought trouble me and keep me awake well into the night.' Richard's eyes reddened. Spittle flecked his beard. 'And why did those people all laugh at you that night after the carnival?'

Noreen smothered his fists with her hands. She spoke calmly.

'Because people are mean and cruel. And you rescued me from them.'

'Yes I did,' said Richard. He got up. 'And those people are laughing at me now.'

Richard searched for truth among the people of Hayle. After all, they had known this young woman longer than he had, and would reveal her secrets and her ways. It was a bad decision. Hayle had never been comfortable with Noreen's virtue and embraced Maggie Bern's stories. Her wicked rumours about Noreen were a public service that punctured the reputation of the virtuous young woman, brought her inflated sense of morality down to earth and released the community from the shadow of her goodness.

It was a mark of his idealistic temperament – and his stupidity – that Richard went to Maggie for the truth.

'Tell me honestly,' he said, leaning over the railings of the Millpond and watching the ducks, 'was there any truth in what you said about my wife?'

'What do you want me to say?' said Maggie. 'You're a married man now.'

'Then don't I deserve the truth more than ever?'

'You may call me a bad woman, Richard. And I will understand that. But I won't be the one to tell you wicked stories about your wife.'

Richard left the meeting lost in a mist of half truths and innuendo; in something not quite graspable yet claustrophobically close. He wondered if Hayle laughed at him. He panicked. But he also came away from the encounter with Maggie marvelling at the complexities and subtleties of the world. Because hadn't the pretty but vulgar Maggie Bern shown a kind of virtue by withholding the full truth? Richard walked home with his head bent and his fist to his mouth. He needed to think it over.

Maggie, meanwhile, sensing the cracks in the marriage, attempted to peer in. Which she did by making frequent and unnecessary errands to the shops, which brought her past the Cankers' window. And past the yard of the Cankers' neighbour Mrs Weeks, a dark-brown old dear wrinkled and ruined by her love for the sun; and perhaps by her appetite for lewd stories.

'It is very sad,' said the old squaw. 'Married six months and they hardly talk to each other.' She squinted up at Maggie. Her nostrils twitched with excitement. 'He calls her all sorts of things.'

'What kind of things?'

'I really couldn't say, dear.'

'Please, Mrs Weeks.'

'Well, all right then. He calls her a harlot and a whore.'

Maggie stepped back and held her hand over her mouth. Mrs Weeks lowered her head and tutted. And it was a shame that two good women couldn't talk about something as innocent as the weather, but instead were forced to discuss the unseemly behaviour of Noreen Canker, nee Penglaze.

It was all well and good for Richard to call Noreen a whore but surely, thought Maggie, proof was needed, or at least some acquaintance with a randy young man. After much thinking and observing the habits of the Canker household, Maggie decided Graham Overton would fit the bill. Or, at least, he would have to do. Graham was a coalman who delivered to Tremeadow Terrace once a week. He was a good-looking chap with sharp cheekbones nicely complemented by a firm jaw.

He was also simple and giggled at anything and everything you said to him. Everyone made fun of him except for Noreen. She stopped to chat with him every Thursday. She was the only person who calmed his giggling, and the pair talked quite normally. Graham would smile and rub the coal dust from his hands, first forming it into tangible strands and then flicking it in the gutter. Sometimes Noreen even brought him indoors for a glass of milk. Graham would emerge a few moments later beaming, his grubby face sporting a brilliant milk moustache.

'Every Thursday she takes him into her bedroom and sucks his thing,' said Maggie.

'Never!' said Mrs Weeks, wrinkling still further a face that seemed wrinkled to full capacity.

'I've seen it with my own eyes,' said Maggie. 'And he leaves great big grubby handprints on the sheets.'

The handprints were a masterful finishing touch. The story swept around Hayle, those prints as good as any evidence. Better even. People started to whisper about Noreen. When she walked through the square the older ones gave disapproving looks and the younger ones giggled. Noreen spent more time hooking her hair behind her ear, her gaze now fixed down on the butts and dirt of the pavement and kerb and not up at the heavenly vistas of yore.

One day after work, George Armstrong took Richard aside. He spoke in quiet, respectful tones, his hand on the cuckolded man's shoulder. When George finished, Richard nodded, thanked him and headed home.

He burst through the door into clammy, steamy warmth and the smell of parsnips and potatoes. Noreen looked around from the pot she was stirring and smiled. Thin licks of hair clung to her temples and her cheeks; she was sweating at the temples.

'You are ruined,' whispered Richard. 'And you've ruined me, too.'

'No, Richard, no. Whatever they say, it isn't true.'

'Hah! You see. In your deceit you go one step too far.' Richard pointed and smiled in triumph. 'How would you know they are saying things? How would you know all about this if it weren't true?'

Noreen dropped her spoon into the pot. She approached Richard. Richard noticed the wide open pores either side of her nose.

'I know that people make up things about me,' said Noreen in a low voice, looking up at Richard.

'But why would they say such wicked things?' said Richard.

Noreen gritted her teeth and looked up at her foolish husband.

'Because I am good and they are wicked.'

Richard stepped away and smiled. It was a stupid, hateful smile: aloof and shiny with saliva.

'So you are better than everyone else are you?' he said.

'Yes,' said Noreen. 'My goodness, yes, I am. At least better than some people. Though I wouldn't call it better, I would call it more honest and good, though it shames me in my vanity to say it. But not as much as it shames the people in this rotten town. That's the truth of it. They are all ashamed of themselves. If only you weren't so bloody stupid, you would see it.'

Richard stepped back. His mouth parted, his tongue hung from his lips like ham from a sandwich. He tried to speak but nothing came. The thing he had feared all of his life had been confirmed; the thing he had suspected, but that had never been spoken of. The thing that he hid away in a dark sanatorium of his mind: it was craning its neck towards the light with squinting, mucky eyes and a shiny grin. It was true. He was stupid. Richard lifted a stupid arm and struck Noreen. Then he did it again, crying out with a howl because he was too stupid for words. Noreen backed away and put her hand to her face. But she didn't cry or make any sound at all.

***

It was the end of Noreen and Richard and they divorced. It was also the end of Noreen. At least this Noreen. She changed over the coming years, so much so that if you could pluck two Noreens from the stream of time and compare them it would be hardly credible to believe that the Noreen of 1937 was the Noreen of 1947, let alone the Noreen of 1997 with her fags and her sherry and her dumb waiter.

Everyone changes, yet the changes in Noreen were so thorough, so complete. And they happened so quickly. Her hair, which had always had a mind of its own unless caressed into submission, became thicker and more unruly, particularly at the top of her head where it formed a crown of fuzz above the rest of her locks. Her skin lost all of its translucent tone and, though it was pink and unblemished, there was nothing delicate about it any more. It looked ordinary, meaty. But her appearance was nothing to her gestures and mannerisms. She rolled her eyes in sympathy at talk of an uncouth husband, she stuck her tongue out with friendly insult, she raised her eyebrows, she tutted, she winked and became such a leading character in that familiar small-town vaudeville of exaggerated responses that every trace of the unique and precious Noreen Canker, nee Penglaze, of yore was soon lost forever.

Soon after Richard left, Maggie visited Mrs Weeks. 'She isn't such a bad sort,' said Maggie as she poured the old dear a cup of tea. Old Mrs Weeks, getting more arthritic and hunched by the day, nodded vaguely and narrowed her eyes at the young tabby from number nine strolling through her parlour.

'But she has gone very sad,' said Maggie, opening a tin of biscuits and handing one to the old dear.

'Very sad,' said Mrs Weeks, forgetting the tabby and wrinkling with worry for Noreen.

And they began to talk about what should be done for Noreen. At first they thought perhaps it best to leave the sad to heal themselves, but later, by the time Maggie had washed the dishes, dried them and put them away, it was thought better to approach Noreen. A few words were put together, something about how a little company can help someone heal.

'After all,' said Maggie, 'we are all in this together.'

And those words lightened the mood in that dark little parlour, and a smile played on lips young and old. And Mrs Weeks said, 'Shall we have another cup of tea?'

And though they were out of biscuits while they drank their second cup, it hardly mattered, because it is a good thing to share your time with a neighbour, and feel the warmth of their company and the happy solace in the thought that, friend or foe, acquaintance or stranger, we are indeed all in this together.

bill's diary

Wednesday 6 March
Steak and chips
Overcast
Thursday 7 March
Fish, boiled potatoes and frozen peas
Bit misty in the morning. Cleared up lovely later
Friday 8 March
Pasty
Bloody awful all day
Saturday 9 March
Bread and butter
Sunny
Val died
Sunday 10 March
One of those Pot Noodles
Sunny
Monday 11 March
Tea and biscuits
Sunny
Tuesday 12 March
Bread and butter, Shredded Wheat
Overcast
Sunday 17 March
Fish and chips with mushy peas
Overcast

EVERY DAY SHE kicked me out she did. After a bit of breakfast and a cup of tea she'd tell me to piss off down to Tommy's and stop making the house untidy. I never saw the point of it all. It's one thing to have a tidy house but a house is for living in and it seems to me she had the cart before the horse making the spick and span of it all more important than my comfort. Funny thing is now she's gone I could leave cups and plates everywhere if I wanted to. Rings on the table too. But I don't. I could sit around the house all day too. But I still go down Tommy's like clockwork. And I don't go home till tea time. Same as if she was still there. Except there's nothing for tea. I might try they ready meals. They deliver to your door too. Bloody great list of meals they have. Hot meals you put straight into the microwave and two minutes, ping, they're ready. Marvellous really. And they won't make any mess because when you're finished you just chuck the plastic tray away. It is marvellous though. I might try they ready meals.

You do look back though don't you. Fifty-odd years. We had a good innings. She had a good innings. I don't expect I'll be far behind her. I expect she's nagging me on the other side telling me to hurry up. But no you shouldn't speak ill of the dead. That's what they say isn't it? And she had a good innings really didn't she?

But you do look back don't you? It seems a long time ago now. Different. I don't mean whether they had microwaves or not. I mean I was different. It's like looking back at another person which I was I suppose because when you learn things you change don't you? And for the worse too. It's like everything you learn doesn't make you wiser it makes you sadder. Better for it if I still thought the way I did when I was a young chap of twenty. I've never known much but you can't help getting older and wiser. Shame really.

My hand is getting sore. Last time I wrote this much was when I complained about that piece of glass we found in that tin of tuna in brine. She put me up to it. I said take the glass out and put the tuna in a roll and if there's still a few crunchy bits well never mind. But she wasn't having that and I had to write a letter to the manufacturers up in bloody Hull. We had a case of tuna in brine. Tuna in bloody rolls or baps for three weeks. I said next time I find a piece of glass in a tin of tuna and brine I'll slit my throat with it. She didn't like that. I suppose it wasn't very nice but you say things don't you?

I can remember the first time I saw her. It was in the Standard. She was a pretty young thing with great big eyes. And skin! You never seen nothing so soft looking. When we started courting I took her up to the dunes. Alive with glowworms it was in the summer evenings. And stars. It makes me bloody morbid to think of it. All those things I said to her. No not me that young man back then because he isn't me. I told her that there was nothing I'd rather do than walk on those dunes with her because it was just me and her in a great big world with the sea out there and all those stars. I don't know. I couldn't describe it then so I never can now. It seems to me the more you know the less you know. And I've forgotten what I mean by that already. Anyway she said she was cold walking on the dunes but that was all right because she nestled up against me, that soft head of hair pushed in against my neck. Or it seemed all right. Only later I realised we weren't two people together in the big world. It was me in the big world and her pushed up against me. She liked a cuddle but she didn't have time for no silliness like the stars and what have you. I don't know if that makes her smarter than me or not.

I loved her I did. I really loved her. And she loved me in her way. But it was a different way. It's hard to describe but it's like we spoke a different language. Because I loved her dearly if she said a kind word to me or squeezed my hand or even smacked my arse while I dried the dishes. But she loved me for different reasons. Sometimes I think she loved me best for packing the bags in the boot of the car at Co-op. I don't know. It's all different than I expected it to be. It's like you grow old on your own and not together. That's what it is. I've put my bloody finger on it now. It's this getting married. You think at last you won't be lonely any more and you even believe it for a while. But in the end it makes no difference no difference at all. But we could have been quite a bit closer when all's said and done.

She liked a party she did. She liked all the gladrags and fancy foods and that. Much more than I did if truth be told. Those blue eyes of hers would light up at a bit of music and dancing and what not. Or at a chap in a fancy suit. She liked the men. Dance with the chaps till her feet were sore she did. One night I put plasters on her bleeding feet for her. Brian Trescothick had been flinging her around all night. She always wore they tight shoes. Used to make me hellish it did. The dancing I mean. It makes me laugh now. I think she was carrying on with Fish Pie Matthews. I saw him feeding fancies into her mouth at Artie Burrow's fortieth birthday party. She was all eyes for him. And she caught my eye just as he was popping one in her mouth. And she watched me as she chewed away and he prattled on to her. Kept her eyes on me for a long time. I never knew what that all meant but she was wrong if she thinks I didn't know they were carrying on. They were carrying on. That weren't no sketching class in St Ives they went to on Thursday nights. Anyway, all water under the bridge now. I didn't mind by then and when she got a bit older all that carrying on stopped. It's amazing what a bit of arthritis will do for your lifestyle. We relied on each other more towards the end. She was company to me and I was company for her. And now she's gone I know how important it is to have a bit of chit chat over this and that. It keeps you human. And even if there isn't any chit chat and you're just watching the box together well it's a comfort to know there's someone there.

I'm sorry Val. I wanted to write down a few words about you and they haven't come out like they should have done. But it doesn't mean anything and you'll know I miss you (and your pasties). Now I know you don't believe in any silliness and I don't go in for churches and vicars but I know there's something out there that has more of an idea what's going on than I do (God help us if there isn't). It's like I used to say to you when we were courting up on the dunes about the world feeling big and small at the same time. I don't know I'll never explain it. It's time to stop. Rest in peace, Val.

Monday 18 March
Two boiled eggs and toast
Rained all day
Tuesday 19 March
Boiled eggs again. Bread instead of toast
Bit blowy
Wednesday 20 March
Two of those Pot Noodles
Overcast
Wasn't feeling hundred percent

the drunken sunset

RONNIE HONEYCHURCH looked up from his painting.

'How much?' he asked the young man again.

'£15,000.'

Ronnie's bald head turned red. His lips began to bubble with words, but nothing came.

'Plus expenses,' said the young man.

This was too much for Ronnie and, dropping his arms hopelessly as if to suggest all the world had gone to hell, he accidentally ran a laden brush from the top to the bottom of his canvas. He stared at his defiled painting. *Bosigren and the Heavens* was no longer flecked with scarlet sunset, but smeared with rude rouge from the sun to the deep blue sea.

'Three weeks' work,' he said in a low, quiet voice, 'and my painting is ruined.'

It was getting dark already. Misty rain swirled in the street. It dripped from the guttering. The young man walked about Ronnie's cluttered studio, his eyes flickering from landscape to landscape, bending his body and leaning his head towards pictures for a closer look, keeping his smart, lint-free black outfit well clear as if the garish oils were still wet and might soil his modernity.

Ronnie looked up from his painting and addressed *Carn Galver in Autumn*. 'But isn't it super? They pay this chap £15,000 for an installation consisting of 42 banana crates.'

'Taken apart and reassembled,' added the young man.

'Oh, yes,' said Ronnie. 'We must give the gentleman credit. Or should I say our credit cards.'

'I find your attitude hostile.'

'How long did it take you?'

'Two days.'

'Did you hear that?' said Ronnie to *Morvah at Dusk*. 'What price art?'

Ronnie stared at the young man. Then he looked away. 'We live in an age,' he said to *Last Rays at Zennor Head*, 'when objects are not judged by their inherent value, but by the fashions of the marketplace.'

'I thought,' said the young man, 'that eternal values went the way of elves, Father Christmas and an interventionist god.'

'Perhaps so, perhaps so,' said Ronnie, gazing at the drunken sunset of his spoiled work. 'And in that case the world is mad and I may as well foul my work – or not.' He shrugged and smiled at the young man.

'It doesn't really matter one way or the other,' said the young man, heading for the door. 'But you might as well.'

And then he was gone.

Ronnie sat on his stool, listening to the dripping rain. It was a grey world out there; a grey, twilight world he hardly knew. The young man had slipped back into it so seamlessly Ronnie would never know him if he passed him on the terrace. In fact so of this bland modern world was the young artist, his very form seemed to scatter in Ronnie's imagination until there was little to distinguish him from the grey particles of dark descending on the awful streets out there.

He thought of winter Penzance and shivered on his stool. It was dark now. He would lock the door soon. Ronnie looked about him at his colourful canvases with oils smeared so thickly one could run one's fingers in the troughs of sunset-bronzed waves. This is art, he thought. And yet he was not stupid. He knew the rudderless tenets of modern art; he knew that cultured people came to laugh and that his customers were the artistically naive. He knew that, after his early successes, his reputation had faded when they discovered he did not paint with irony but with that most gauche of all artistic approaches: sincerity. All the same, thought Ronnie, this is art.

He looked at his *Drunken Sunset*. 'And this,' he said, 'is not.'

***

'I don't care what you say, Ronnie,' said corpulent, creaseless Roger Maddern. He pointed at Ronnie's *Drunken Sunset*. 'This is marvellous.'

'It's an abomination,' said Ronnie.

'Not at all. It's a step forward.' Roger shook the pasty in his hand and showered Ronnie in flakes of pastry. 'Your sunset sliding like that into the sea. Do you know what it says to me?'

Ronnie shook his head.

'You'll like this,' said Roger. He belched, his powdery red cheeks bloating for a moment. 'It says: "I am the sun and it's been a long day and I – am – absolutely – bloody – knackered."'

'Oh my goodness. It says all that, does it?'

Roger licked a chubby finger and attended to a speck on his flawless, deep blue suit.'

'It's what I would call expressive. You have gone beyond, Ronnie, merely representing the world about you to…' Roger crushed his pasty in his fist. 'To... imbibing it… with emotion.'

'Whose emotion?' said Ronnie.

'Whose?' said Roger. 'What does it matter whose? It's emotional, that's all.'

Ronnie slid off his stool and began to pace back and forth. 'Well, it's my emotion in that… thing. And what if it says, "I am the smeared sun. I am nature and values defiled by the myopic hubris of popular trends and fashion."' Ronnie clambered back up on his stool. '"I am the start of something insidious. I am that which will herald the end of all culture."' And though he grinned his face was red and sweat trickled down his temples.

Roger bit into his pasty and peered closely at the painting. 'No I think you're mistaken, Ronnie. I can't see that at all.' He popped the last of his pasty into his mouth and brushed his lapels. 'Anyway, I must get back to the office and you owe me two month's rent.' He paused on the threshold. 'Come to think of it, I have a sneaking suspicion Sheila would be very taken with your sunset. How does £50 sound?'

'Never,' said Ronnie, 'It is worthless.'

'After all I've done for you, too. Do you know how hard I had to twist Terence Gulliver's arm to get you your exhibition? You should never have had it if I wasn't his landlord.'

'I know, Roger, and it's very good of you. But the answer is still no.'

'All right then, £75.'

Ronnie stabbed a brush towards the painting. 'I would not sell this… thing… for all the money in the world.'

'Suit yourself.' Roger winked at Ronnie. 'By the way, did you say your painting was worthless – or priceless?'

And with that he was gone, back into the rainy grey.

***

The garish golds and rouges of Ronnie Honeychurch's work are a slander on our landscape. If Mr Honeychurch paints a simple tree it must be adorned with a slither of sunset pink, like flesh through the slip of a skirt; if gorse should be in flower, watch out – its golds will jangle across Mr Honeychurch's landscapes like so much cheap jewellery. In Mr Honeychurch's work, even an austere moorland takes on a suggestive, garish leer, as if it would welcome you to sample the fleshpots hidden beneath its grey boulders. In short, Mr Honeychurch makes a brothel madam out of our beautiful Penwith landscape.

The newspaper shook and crackled in Ronnie's hands. He threw it on the desk and looked about him at his paintings. Suddenly the world seemed small and claustrophobic and the exhibition moments away. He began to pace the studio. Never before had local critic and collector Adrian Goldsworthy attacked his works so. With the disaster came indignity, too: the vicious words appeared only as an afterthought in a review of another artist's work. Another artist, incidentally, who painted Ronnie's landscape in swathes of murky grey – all steel seas and concrete-hued boulders – and who was praised for the unblinking truth of barren, spinster January.

Ronnie stopped and looked at *Watchcroft at Sundown*. He was still shaking and his voice trembled as he spoke. 'And why is it that my beloved Penwith Moor must be a woman, whore or humble cottage dweller, and not just my beloved Penwith Moor?' To think that the critic should find the truth in a gloomy and narcissistic interpretation of reality and not in reality itself, which is all Ronnie plainly and humbly represented as best he could.

He continued to stalk the studio, his short legs moving swiftly and soundlessly on the wooden floor. He began to doubt himself, looking from one painting to another, examining his reds and his oranges and his pinks and wondering if the sun did indeed set more than once a day in his world. He came up close to a painting and peered at the deep buttery yellows of his gorse, the buds so swollen with colour they shone at dusk like little lamps. Then he examined several of his crumbling engine houses, which were never knotted or arthritic but always luxuriantly clad in glossy ivy and showered with wild flowers. He dropped his hands on a table and stared into the wood, thinking of the exhibition again, of the first major display of his work in 12 years, and of the crowds who would judge him. For a moment he believed that Goldsworthy was right. And yet these paintings, they were what Ronnie saw. And, by God, they were what anyone could see.

Hurrying over to the old mahogany chest, Ronnie opened the top drawer, snatched a pile of photographs and spread them on the table. He examined landscapes at Carn Galver, Bosigren, Zennor, Pendeen, Botallack, Watchcroft, Levant; and details – flowers, insects, stones, grass, cows, goats, boulders, engine houses, seagulls.

He picked up a photo and held it close to his eyes, scrutinising not just the colours and the composition but the creases and frayed edges. Then another and another, holding them close this way, his eyes darting about the image as if by looking hard enough he would see it perfectly, as it really was.

He came to the very last photo at the bottom of the pile. Her. Head thrown upwards, laughing, but still those black eyes fixed on Ronnie through tangles of dark curly hair. The world around her was so vivid, so blue and yellow and green and yet she was so monochrome with her pale face and her simple black dress. She looked superimposed, as if she did not belong there at all; as if she might walk away from that scene at any moment.

Ronnie lifted his hand and ran his fingers across his head, combing back the hair that was long a memory now. He did it often at the thought of her, and the shock of its absence never diminished after all these years. He patted at the fluff about his ears, that feathery nest that held his bald head like an egg, and smiled as he always smiled at the thought of that smooth dome, his small, sharp eyes, disappearing as his mouth grew.

Oh, to be sure Ronnie was no less serious than he had been in the old days when his brow had furrowed so fiercely under licks of brown hair. He was more serious, in fact: and yet there comes a point with seriousness when there is nothing left but laughter. At least in company.

Ronnie gathered the photos together, placing her on the bottom again, and returned them to the chest of drawers. As he crossed the room he saw his *Drunken Sunset* propped up against a table leg. He stared at it contemptuously. Though he had taken it from its easel and relegated it to this corner of the studio, three customers had made appreciative noises about the accidental scene and two had even offered to buy it. He remembered the enthusiastic and intelligent words of one gentleman who wished to purchase the painting, and how his own voice quivered as he politely informed him it was not for sale. Ronnie continued to stare at the canvas. The air whistled up and down his nostrils. He thought first about his exhibition, then about Penwith Moor, his inspiration for a life's work. A place to which he wished never to return. A place, in fact, he had not visited for 30 years.

***

The following day Ronnie stepped into the misty wet, a red cagoule wrapped tight around his head and a rucksack on his back. He hurried down Market Jew Street towards the bus station. A washed-out scene, it was, the air thick with fine rain, the street a blur. Only the Woolworths sign offered hope, the hard red font shining like an emergency exit, offering temporary escape from January Penzance. And from Penwith Moor. Ronnie pulled the toggles tighter around his head.

He got on a bus to St Just. There he changed buses and headed on the coast road to St Ives. The windows steamed up; even in those places one could see through, the scene was broken into pieces by the beads of rain that clung to the panes. Ronnie saw a blur of blue sky and brown hedgerows, the moving silhouettes of engine houses circling the bus as it twisted through the narrow lanes, bursts of granite. As the bus passed through Trewellard, the sky lit up and the little drops clinging to the windows turned gold for a moment before sinking back to grey.

Ronnie got off the bus at Morvah and walked along the road to Carn Galver. He reached the hill and began to walk up slowly, his cagoule and waterproof trousers swishing and his feet slapping through the little river running down the path. He stopped several times to adjust the rucksack, staring into the river and concentrating hard on evenly balancing the weight between his shoulders. As he got closer to the top he stopped again and double-knotted his laces, to keep them well clear of the muddy ground.

He reached the top and looked about him at the landscape. He looked at the ocean, at the moors rolling towards St Just on one side and St Ives on the other, at the granite erupting from the earth. The sky was getting lighter, the grey breaking up into pockets of blue and swirling white. Ronnie lay his rucksack on a rock and took out a camera and a sketch book. He began to take pictures and to sketch, keeping his gaze from the wider landscape and losing himself in details: textures, grass, flowers. He worked fast, as if he would get the job done as quickly as possible, get enough material for the exhibition and then return to his studio. He knelt close to the ground to take a picture of a piece of curved purple granite no bigger than his hand poking through the earth. He smelled the damp, fruity odour of the ground.

And then it came: the thing he knew would come somehow or other. In a moment his olfactory senses transported him and he was 30 years younger and in love. He felt the ghost of his old self within him, still alive somewhere. And then it was gone. Ronnie felt dizzy. He pushed himself up from the ground and sat on a nearby boulder.

'Golly,' he said, and he looked around him, grinning into the landscape, pretending to see everything as he scanned from left to right, but trying to see nothing. And yet still he saw that day so many years ago and he saw today and he knew that the two worlds were utterly different. More different than he could ever have believed. For one day, that day, as he gripped her to him, the objects of the universe – the rocks, the flowers, the clouds in the blue sky, the ocean – all had throbbed and crackled with the beautiful, terrible clarity of truth. Love had made him a part of God, and he saw – in flashes – everything as it truly was; all was connected and placed just so because the universe was just so. Love had infected everything. Even photos.

And yet today those very same objects, this very same landscape, was a desultory affair. Rocks were strewn haphazardly, without reason; they were stranded, lonely objects that knew nothing of a universe that knew nothing of them. A bleakness infected the scene, a godlessness, an obscureness and forgetfulness, as if the universe was composed of nothing more that an infinite number of isolated moments and there were no befores and no afters. There were no analogies, no reverberations, no echoes and no poetry: all life was summed up by a mute, cold boulder, sitting, for no reason at all, in a mute cold landscape.

'You fool,' said Ronnie quietly. 'You poor fool. You have pickled and jarred yourself just as you pickled and jarred that day 30 years ago. And it is all a lie.'

And it was a lie. For how could Ronnie believe in the immutable nature of his landscape, his art, when that summer, which had been full of the golden light of long days, had ended so sadly, so bleakly? And this belief in the eternal moment, how it had aged Ronnie – this lonely, little man with his seething smiles, his little pink head and his beard. This absurd little man. What a trick it was to believe only in the day and not the dusk. And yet somehow he knew about this day, this new day – he had known about it for 30 years.

Ronnie got up from his boulder and stumbled down the hill. He looked around him, hardly knowing where to go next. The landscape he had painted for 30 years was a foreign land. Then he grinned. He had an idea. The tears welled up in his eyes.

'We shall see,' said Ronnie. 'We shall see.' And he began to laugh at the bleak world about him because in a world that was so alien, so lacking in bearings, laughter in the wake of pain was as appropriate as tears.

He walked through the narrow lanes towards St Ives. It was getting dark. The things of the universe came and went: dark hills, cows' silhouettes, occasional cars hissing in the rain, their headlights sliding over the stray revelations of the present moment – thickets of bramble, rivers of water, road signs. Ronnie saw it all come and go but mostly he was lost in thoughts of love and failure.

He knew that the art world, well this small outpost of it at least, had despised him because he believed in the truth of things. Not the truth of a magnificent world sucked into greedy eyes and subjected to the phantasmagoria of the mind. Not in the kind of truth that makes a tinpot god of man, but the truth that is God in all things, that is vital in all things, in things beyond art: especially in things beyond art. He was hopelessly old fashioned and always had been.

'And yet you shall be free, Ronnie, you shall be free,' he said. And he walked with purpose, because he walked the natural path of his sorrow. And it was the evening following a sad day 30 years ago and there were no intervening years at all.

After half an hour or so he passed the Gurnard's Head pub and soon after he reached Zennor. He stood in the little square between the church and the pub. Laughter from the pub spilled into the dark, damp night. Ronnie walked in. He ordered a drink and sat down by the fire. A cat jumped on his lap. He recognised a few faces from the old days, but no one recognised him. Why would they? Ronnie looked so different now. He wondered why he had come at all, why a universe that was so emphatically different to the one he had lived in and painted should oblige him now. He saw that the narratives, the stories we create to connect the present to the past are not threads, but cobwebs: beautiful and fine but so inconsequential the world walks through them as if they are not there.

Ronnie stroked the cat's head, then rubbed his own head and grinned. A group of people at a table nearby stared at him. Ronnie was an odd fellow. It was better off if he stayed in his studio, just as he had done for most of the last 30 years. He finished his drink, gently lifted the cat and dropped it by the fire. Then he buttoned up his coat and stepped out of the pub into the night.

It had stopped raining. The night was still. Ronnie looked across the way at the church. Orange lights underlit the building and in the glow he could see the little sheltered spots in the graveyard they had embraced on evenings long ago, and the rough Cornish crosses they had stroked with their hands. He remembered how she would examine her palms afterwards and frown at the white scratches. He loitered for some time, because he knew he would never come here again. He began to think of the long walk over the moors back to Penzance when he heard a quick tick tick tick that soon swelled into a clop clop clop. A woman was coming down the hill next to the church and heading for the pub. She stepped into the light of the square, her face tilted down, her hands pulling up the collar of her coat around her neck to keep out the cold. She altered her course to walk around Ronnie, but she did not acknowledge him. Then she entered the pub and was gone.

He had barely seen a face in the dim light, but those quick, irritated steps and the hunched gait – it was just the way she had walked on winter nights, a creature who emphatically refused to dawdle or know the cold. Ronnie began to hope, then to believe. Because that sound, it echoed through the years despite everything, despite a landscape that had disappeared and a man that had disappeared. It was an echo hidden in the folds of darkness and it thrilled Ronnie. For if the cold white light of present day was so ruthlessly unsentimental, did the past take refuge in the night?

Again time and distance melted away and Ronnie was with her 30 years ago, following just behind to join her for a drink because she always walked so fast in the cold. He hesitated. He knew, he absolutely knew now what was happening inside. She was taking off her coat and flinging it on the floor next to the bar. She was sitting down at the end stall, frowning and pressing her hands on the cheek of any neighbour – man or woman – to show them how cold she was. Finally her pale face was unfurling and she was turning her head from one end of the room to the other, smiling with that wonderful warmth that says I am here now, I am warm and all is right with the world. It made Ronnie dizzy – almost sick – to think of the thousand nights he had missed the smile that made all the world just as it should be.

He stepped slowly towards the door, hardly knowing when or who he was as he approached the glass. And then he saw her. And though afterwards he wondered if it had been her at all, and even dreamed he had been mistaken and chuckled so heartily at his mistake he woke himself up, the woman he had loved so intensely was metres and moments away from him now. She sat on the stool, just as he knew she would. But her face was puffier and her features, which had once so bewitchingly conspired together, seemed lonely things. Her mouth had dropped a little lower, her eyes were smaller and sunken behind her cheeks. Cheeks that were once exotically high but were now wide and barren. What she was had faded away. She seemed indifferent, and flashed with her former intensity only when sucking on a cigarette, her eyebrows digging downwards, her lids lowered towards mouth, all her powers now directed towards roll-up. Ronnie remembered how those lips had curled, pushing up fine cheeks towards black eyes that sparkled darkly at the thought of some artistic megalomania, and he saw now those same features come to life only as she made herself a slave to simple desires. This woman, this beautiful, talented, vain woman who had been so powerfully in concert with herself, who had held the universe in concert, who had destroyed Ronnie, was clinging on to what was left through endless cigarettes in the cramped amber cabin of a pub, a small precarious vessel on a great ocean of night.

Ronnie stared and stared and one or two people began to look but she did not. He wondered if he should try to talk to her, to understand, find solace with her, perhaps even smile at the past and laugh at the intervening years. But it was hopeless. He would get no answer because the woman he had loved was not there any more.

'And perhaps,' thought Ronnie, 'just perhaps, she was never there at all.'

And he turned away and walked into the night, chuckling at the great joke he had played upon himself for 30 years.

*** *

'Ronnie, what on earth are you doing?' said Roger.

Ronnie pulled his hands out of a bucket of black paint and waved them at his friend.

'Today is a black day, and so on to the canvas it goes.'

'But I can hardly see your landscapes anymore.'

'Tomorrow, Roger, there is always tomorrow. But today we are black.' And Ronnie grinned, for although he had felt a little gloomy that morning, the synchronicity of mood and art lifted his spirits. And it was a beautiful, sunny day.

'I don't know, Ronnie, I think you're taking this all too far.' Roger lumbered about the studio, squinting at Ronnie's pictures. 'A bit of fun with paint is one thing. But where will this lead?'

'There is only one place where this can lead, my friend. But you shall have to wait and see.'

'Well, I'm not standing around waiting to find out. It's a fine day and the bakery's got six cream horns for the price of four.'

'Cream horns! Lovely!'

'I am going to sit in Morrab Gardens, watch the fountain and eat myself silly.'

'And I,' said Ronnie wiping his black hands on his overalls, 'am going to join you.'

'I say, Ronnie,' said Roger. 'I'm not sure about the new direction, but you do seem cheerful.'

'I am cheerful. And I am almost ready for the exhibition. And do you know what, Roger? If the cakes are exceedingly good, I might splash a little white on *Watchcroft in January* in honour of the cream inside.'

'I wish you wouldn't, Ronnie,' said Roger, as they strolled out into the sunshine. 'But I must say I am glad to see you so happy.'

***

Ronnie was happy. So happy he began to smile and then chuckle at the slightest provocation. On one occasion he was quietly mixing his paints and the thought of Roger's alarm at his recent work tickled him so he spilt fleshy pink all over *The Crowns at Sunrise*. This delighted Ronnie. Nothing seemed to happen now that didn't find its way into a painting.

This productive, happy period had begun just days after he returned from Penwith Moor. Ronnie had sat in his studio, gloomily looking at the paintings around him, fearing ever more the gallery show, the scathing reviews that would finish him as an artist. Ronnie paced the studio for days. He had visions of himself among the tourist industry painters in St Ives, and the gaudy clownery of it all horrified him. Then one day he opened the bottom drawer of the dresser and picked out the picture of her. And, yes, the picture had changed – she had changed. Somehow that vision through glass a few days earlier had infected the past and this perfect image of beauty seemed corrupted by what was to come. Already there was that barrenness about her cheeks and a tapering at her eyes as if all the sucked cigarettes of her middle years were known to her face back then. There was a diabolical trick at play in the soul of mankind, thought Ronnie, that made men and women chain themselves to things – to times and places – that did not exist anymore, that perhaps did not exist even when they appeared to.

Ronnie buried the picture in the drawer and paced about the studio, a terrible anger rising up in him until he pulled at his beard, kicked at stools and cursed his paintings. He saw the *Drunken Sunset* and stopped. And smiled. The air hissed through his teeth. How wonderfully that sun oozed into the sea. It was not Roger's contented evening. It was the day bleeding into night. It was time, place and memory bleeding into darkness – into nothingness.

'And all it needs,' said Ronnie, is some blue, a thin layer of light blue to bring a bloodless chill over that moor and it really will look super.'

This was the start. Ronnie painted with his fingers, and with a freedom he had never known. No more squinting into the past, brush poised, searching out the ghosts of old feelings – Ronnie felt the cold anger at his fingertips as he thinned out his blue and smeared on the paint. He turned his attention to other paintings. By applying a mixture of thinners and turpentine to canvas he broke down the hard paint. Then he ran his fingers over his work. Forms melted: boulders, sky and gorse began to merge. Not in some reassuring association of objects, but in a disastrous way, for the essence of an object was lost in contact with another. It was turmoil. Boulder lost itself in sky, sky was infected by boulder. The world on canvas collapsed in a whirl of anger. It delighted Ronnie. For the first time as an artist he was not a slave to an imagined object or place, but a creator, forming new worlds that were powerful because they were true, even if only for a moment in time.

By 5 o'clock he had reworked half his canvases. It was a good day.

'How ya doin'?' An American voice. An elderly couple ducked into the doorway, looking about them and smiling ostentatiously, preparing to be charmed by regional arts and handicrafts.

'Greetings!' said Ronnie, smeared from head to toe in a mixture of colours, but mainly the browny hue of merged paints. 'Welcome to my little world!'

They stared at him, then at his paintings. What a dreadful trick to be promised a local artist at work and be confronted, at best, by some art therapy patient left to his own devices, at worst, a madman. Yes a madman. Ronnie watched with amusement as they backed out of the door with appeasing grins. They could have been no more shocked if he had smeared the world with his excrement. And if he had done, would that be art? Was everything art? Was the artist the child at play with his own excrement because there is no parent left in the world to watch him? And Ronnie chuckled and continued in his happy anger until nine.

***

The Gokyneth Gallery was a white, cavernous space.

Voices echoed from its walls and footsteps squeaked on its floors as if it did not want your words and actions and would thrust them back at you. Ronnie's paintings hung stranded on the walls, whirls of colour that meant nothing yet, because no one had ascribed them with meaning. People clung to each other in little groups that reflected schools and tendencies. This was common. Meaning and truth were relative in this world and relationships were all; Ronnie's paintings were like strangers at a party in need of a good introduction.

Ronnie listened to the chatter echoing around the gallery, and wondered at the trivial conversations. Soon he ignored it and moved from painting to painting, Roger at his side. It was crucial to know if his work would be a success or a failure. Art was vital and alive to Ronnie in a way it never had been before. After all, what is art in the shadow of gods but merely an imitation of the divine? But in this world it is the solace and the truth of mankind. He felt an urgency within him, an irritated energy that made him pull at his beard and smooth his head and move from one through to the next with alarming rapidity, as if he were catching up for a lifetime of immobility. He felt instinctively that he spoke the truth, a new disturbing truth that he must share.

'I'll give you this,' said Roger Maddern, pulling the head off a tiger prawn and nodding towards Ronnie's paintings. 'They are absolutely nothing like your previous work.' He popped the prawn into his mouth and chewed. 'Where's that one I like?'

Ronnie pointed to a swirl of blue and green.

'What happened to the sun?' said Roger.

'It set,' said Ronnie, peering from one canvas to the next.

The evening really got going with the arrival of collector and literary critic Adrian Goldsworthy. He strode in wearing green corduroy trousers, a paisley waistcoat, a yellow shirt and curly blond hair short at the sides and high on top of his head. Though influential in local arts circles, Mr Goldsworthy cast an absurd figure to the uneducated and culturally illiterate, who did not know that his apparel was a nod to American artist Mark Rothko, and who thought of him generally as a rather serious-looking clown. Of course his choice of costume was a brave reaction to that tendency among many men in arts circles to wear muted colours, often black, and words such as 'brave' and 'uncompromising' were often used to describe him by his peers, which went a long way to mitigate the frequent 'twats' he endured from the local ignorati as he strode down Market Jew Street. There was not a twat to be heard as he strode into the gallery, nodded at friends and acquaintances and began to examine the paintings.

'Expressionist tendencies?' he asked himself as he gazed at *Carn Galver at Sunset*, before moving on. 'Joan Miro – the murder of painting!' he said, pointing and wagging his finger at a blur of colours. Mr Goldsworthy squinted as he walked around and even seemed unsure once or twice in which direction to turn. But then out of nowhere came one of his ejaculations – 'Piero Manzoni! Faeces!' – and he would steer towards a painting. He was a man on a search, an odyssey, trying to find his bearings in abstract shapes and swirling, ever changing meanings; and though at times he seemed hopelessly lost and discouraged, all at once he would cry out at what he believed to be a cultural reference point, like a sailor lost in a bank of fog shouting in hoarse delight as navigable stars briefly broke through.

All the while, a small crowd followed. Ronnie stayed close by his enemy, praying for the approval that would make a success of his latest work, but also muttering darkly through his grin as the critic tried to do what so many critics do: bludgeon a work with words and concepts until they are quite sure it has stopped breathing.

'Just see it,' said Ronnie. 'See it, then be done with it.'

Roger Maddern, meanwhile, was absently shelling prawns and looking scandalised at the strange ejaculations of Mr Goldsworthy.

'He's got some neck, Ronnie. If he doesn't like your paintings, that's his prerogative. But all this effing and blinding.' Roger looked around for his fellow scandalised, but found nothing but admiring acolytes.

After Adrian Goldsworthy finished his tour, he talked to a small group of acquaintances. Ronnie was on the receiving end of a few smiles and nods and the odd grinning 'wonderful', but for the most part he and Roger were left alone. Ronnie was devastated. He knew he should not care for the opinions of these people, but from who else could an artist hope for the understanding that makes this life more than a realm of shadows and ghosts and half-heard phrases and tongues that loll and grope for meaning but fail, fail, fail every time until every man and woman is abandoned to their loneliness? Ronnie had spoken and their was truth in his work, albeit an ephemeral one. And yet nobody listened.

'So these are your friends, eh?' said Roger.

'Oh, my goodness,' said Ronnie. 'I wouldn't call them that.'

'I should think not. They haven't given you the time of bloody day.' Roger put his hand on Ronnie's shoulder. 'Artists? Give me the other type of artist any day. You know, Ronnie, the one you get in pubs. What do you say to a quiet pint in The Union?'

Ronnie agreed, and was beginning to look for the

least embarrassing path to the exit when he felt a hand on his shoulder.

'Absolutely spellbinding.'

He turned around.

Adrian Goldsworthy stood before him.

'From your Halcyon landscapes, that lovely wilful naivety of your early and middle period, to this!' Adrian Goldsworthy pointed at the paintings about him one by one. 'To this and this and this and this!'

A spellbinding little speech it was. And in the absence of any considered appraisal, Adrian Goldsworthy's repetitions got to the very essence, to the this-ness, of Ronnie's paintings.

And already the crowd was gazing at the walls, some grinning and nodding knowingly at Ronnie's this-ness and at the skilful way he had avoided blundering into the gaucherie of that-ness.

Adrian Goldsworthy raised his glass. 'All that remains is to toast the man of the hour. To your health, Ronnie.'

'To your health,' said the crowd, gathered around little Ronnie, raising glasses as one.

Ronnie looked at the raised glasses that shined and tinkled above him. I will remember this forever, he thought. The years came to him in flashes. He remembered a summer's day long ago sitting against a dry stone hedge on the moors with a bottle of wine; a time when he could feel all the world in the warmth of the late afternoon sun and all the universe, a tangible universe, flow from his pencil. He remembered his middle years in the gallery, how he had given up the vital moment of creation for a kind of history-making and then he thought of his recent work. And it was while the most recent canvases shifted in his mind that Ronnie realised he was looking at something quite beautiful.

Through the raised glasses, his paintings turned ruby red and twisted into strange and unusual shapes. Changing already. At once he thought of the glass door at the Tinner's Arms and her. Ronnie felt his brows darken and so he began to grin. He looked at the faces surrounding him and of course they did not see those paintings change – did not know they must change. And his happiness was tempered by an anger and contempt for these people fawning over him and his paintings because they understood nothing of his work, nothing of what he was trying to say at all, knew nothing even of the truth of the moment, let alone that the truth of the moment had passed.

Once accepted, understood, he was anxious to throw his work away and move on to greater things. And what greater things there would be! Ronnie clenched his fists and felt the muscles in his arm stiffen. He felt angry and inspired all at once.

'What a journey, Ronnie' said Adrian Goldsworthy. 'What can I say but that in this humble critic's opinion you have arrived?'

'Ooh,' said Ronnie, grinning, his small sharp eyes flashing at the crowd of people surrounding him.

'Arrived? Super!' And he pretended to open a door and get out of a vehicle. 'Well, I'd better have a look around.'

And Ronnie did have a look around and already there were little orange stickers on several of his paintings.

'I had to have your *Drunken Sunset* for myself,' said Adrian Goldsworthy later. 'It has a – how shall I say – it has a certain… a certain…'

'It certainly does, doesn't it,' said Ronnie. He frowned. 'And yet it is not quite finished.'

'What do you mean?'

'Nothing of consequence. It just seems to me these days that the very world is shifting under our feet. In such a world aren't we lying a little to ourselves if we consider anything truly finished or completed?'

Adrian Goldsworthy began to nod. He scanned from left to right, as if looking for something, but settled instead on a bit more nodding, more vigorous this time, as if to demonstrate that he understood what Ronnie said better than anyone – even Ronnie.

'Postmodern,' he said finally. 'Purely postmodern.'

'Is it?' said Ronnie. 'Super! But I don't know all about that. It just occurred to me that it would be a blessed relief for the artist – and the purest artistic statement, in fact – if something became nothing.'

'Post postmodern?' said Adrian Goldsworthy.

Ronnie ignored him and grinned. He seemed lighter all of a sudden, as if he had stumbled on a marvellous idea.

'After all,' he said, 'what is more pure than nothing?' And, as if brilliantly demonstrating Ronnie's thesis, trumping Ronnie, in fact, Adrian Goldsworthy stared at him for a long time and said absolutely nothing at all. When he did speak, it was a little later. And privately to Ronnie.

'Just to clarify, the painting is mine now?'

'Why of course, Adrian.'

'You see, I like it as it is. And you said you had more work to do.'

'A discreet signature, that kind of thing. Details.'

On the way home, Roger said, 'Do you know, Ronnie, I don't think I've ever seen you so happy.'

'And do you know, Roger, I don't think I have ever been so happy. At least not for a long, long time.'

'The sales is it? The thought of all those spondoolicks?'

'Oh, no, Roger! It is something far more important. For the first time in a very long time I feel fully at one with my work.'

And Ronnie, in the most peculiar expression of joy, threw out his arms, jumped into the air and looked up into the sky.

'You're a funny man, Ronnie. But I'll tell you this – when I get home I'll also be at one. At one with a great big cream bun.'

***

'And that,' said Roger cutting open his pasty, 'is the last I saw of him.'

Sheila loaded her fork and filled her mouth. 'Where do you think he might have gone to?'

'I have no idea. He did have a bit of stuff once. A long time ago.'

'Never mind how long ago. A man will follow a woman to the ends of the earth.'

Roger pointed his fork at his wife. 'And if she makes pasties like you do, he'll be bloody right to.'

They laughed. Then they settled into their pasties, heads down and in a sublime middle distance of pastry and potato and chuck steak.

Sheila leaned back in her chair for a break.

'Hey, but what about it though? Burning all of his paintings.'

Roger leaned back too. 'But did you know, Sheila, he sent every person who bought one a little pot – like an urn – full of the ashes? It was in today's paper.'

Sheila shook her head.

'No I didn't know that, but it doesn't surprise me. I did like Ronnie, I liked him very much. But he was highly strung.'

'But this is the best bit. Do you know what that twa… that nincompoop in the paper said?'

'He was all for it, was he?'

Roger put down his knife and fork and reached into his breast pocket. He unfolded a page of newspaper and began to read.

In an ideal world Ronnie Honeychurch would have presented us each with an invoice for his work – and nothing else. For that would have represented the pure abstraction he was searching for. In the circumstances, he did the next best thing and made a sly dig at the collectors who will believe in the myth of perfectly manifested objects. He presented us each with a little urn of our painting's ashes. I will say it now and I will say it loudly and clearly: Ronnie Honeychurch is a genius and I gladly pay £3,000 for a pot of ashes.

Roger put the paper away. 'Now, my dear, what do you think of that?'

'I don't know quite what to think. It's giving me indigestion. But I do know one thing – some people have got more money than sense.'

'Exactly. I'll tell you this for nothing: when people stray too far from the essentials of life – like filling their cakeholes – they're likely to get into all sorts of trouble.'

And if filling your cakehole was a route to happiness, Roger and Sheila were Epicureans of the highest order, happily masticating and mixing saliva with pastry and vegetables with absolutely no trouble at all.

'I don't think we'll ever see Ronnie again, do you?' said Sheila.

'No, I don't,' said Roger. 'But life goes on.'

He popped the last of his pasty into his mouth.

'But what about it, eh? Burning your paintings! What kind of artist burns his paintings?'

'I have absolutely no idea.' Sheila got up. 'But I do know a man who'd like a bit of homemade apple tart for afters.'